saints of augustine

P. E. Ryan

An Imprint of HarperCollins*Publishers*

HarperTeen is an imprint of HarperCollins Publishers.
Saints of Augustine
Copyright © 2007 by P. E. Ryan
All rights reserved.
Printed in the United States of America.

Library of Congress Cataloging-in-Publication Data
Ryan, Patrick, 1965–
    Saints of Augustine / P. E. Ryan. — 1st ed.
        p.   cm.
    Summary: In St. Augustine, Florida, former best friends
Charlie Perrin and Sam Findley, now both sixteen, come to
realize that their friendship is the only thing that will keep
them afloat when each of their worlds is turned upside
down through death, divorce, and the seemingly out-of-
control direction of their lives.
    ISBN-10: 0-06-085810-9 (trade bdg.)
    ISBN-13: 978-0-06-085810-0 (trade bdg.)
    ISBN-10: 0-06-085811-7 (lib. bdg.)
    ISBN-13: 978-0-06-085811-7 (lib. bdg.)
    [1. Best friends—Fiction. 2. Friendship—Fiction.
3. Conduct of life—Fiction. 4. Self acceptance—Fiction.
5. Homosexuality—Fiction. 6. Death—Fiction. 7. Saint
Augustine (Fla.)—Fiction.] I. Title.
PZ7.R9555Sai 2007   2006019519
[Fic]—dc22   CIP
                                                   AC

Typography by Joel Tippie
1 2 3 4 5 6 7 8 9 10
❖
First Edition

17

To Beverly Neel

acknowledgments

Many thanks to my editor, Tara Weikum, whose wisdom and tireless guidance helped shape this novel in so many ways, and to my agent, Lisa Bankoff, for her enthusiasm and sharp eye, and for getting the manuscript into the right hands.

Thanks also to Michael Carroll, Donnie Conner, and Ann Patchett for their friendship, faith, and endless encouragement.

I'm also indebted to Ron Duran for his technical assistance and to Joe B. McCarthy for his assistance in technically fine-tuning certain aspects of this novel.

Finally, as always, immeasurable thanks to Fred Blair.

1.

Beyond the passenger window, the palm scrub ended abruptly and the Atlantic opened like a vast, blue-green desert. Charlie took his eyes off the road long enough to watch a pair of pelicans gliding above the surface of the ocean, side by side. They hovered against the wind for a moment; then one of them dove straight into the water, creating a splash of white foam that vanished before the bird broke the surface again. Was it holding a fish in its beak? He couldn't tell. The other pelican kept flying, without looking back.

My car, Charlie thought as he sailed north on A1A, *is my best friend in the world.*

This was immediately followed by the thought *How pathetic is that?*

Still, if you had to have a car for a best friend, you could do worse. Charlie's was a bright red 1974 Volkswagen Bug, built fifteen years before he was even born, and it was in prime condition. Bone leather interior, whitewall tires, and a shiny chrome bumper he kept polished so that the sun glinted off of it. Best of all was the fact that he'd bought the car himself with the money he'd saved up over the past two summers. All those hours in the heat, getting eaten alive by mosquitoes while he brushed primer and paint onto other people's houses, had actually amounted to something. He'd spent almost everything he had on the car, and it felt like a reward— not just for working so hard, but for getting through what he hoped was the worst year of his life.

He pictured himself telling this to Bob Costas on HBO: *You know, I was in a low spot when I was fifteen. My mom had just died, and that was rough, really rough. And I thought, I've got to do something, I've got to get focused or I'll go crazy. So I became obsessed with the idea of saving up for a car. I worked hard, saved my money; and a year later, I was sitting behind the wheel.*

The interview would move from there to the humongous contract he'd just signed with the Miami Heat.

For now, he felt—and looked—like anything *but* a pro basketball star. There were paint smears on his T-shirt. His hands stank of linseed oil, and his fingernails were encrusted with glazing compound. His dark hair, he saw when he glanced at himself in the rearview mirror, was sticking up in sweat-glued spikes. He'd been working on the Danforth house since nine o'clock that morning, and his workday was finally over. He ran a grimy finger around the dial on the radio, found a song he liked, and turned it up.

It's not easy being a sports celebrity, he'd tell Costas. *There's a lot of pressure that comes with a multimillion-dollar contract. Sometimes I wish I could just go back to being that simple guy driving his VW around St. Augustine, not a care in the world.*

As if he didn't have cares. He had plenty. In fact, he was up to his neck in them.

Near the outskirts of town, he came up on the first wave of motels and souvenir shops and tourist traps—places he hardly noticed, being a local. Today, though, he noticed Gatorland because a girl was coming out of the front door, and she was *fine*. She had strawberry-blond hair and wore a tight yellow shirt and a pair of shorts cut so high, it was practically a bathing-suit bottom. Her legs weren't very tan— she was probably a tourist. Which would make sense, because why else would she be holding a bag from the Gatorland gift shop? They sold nothing but Florida junk in there. Alligator back scratchers. Plastic banks shaped like space shuttles. He imagined pulling up in front of the shop and offering her a personal tour of the town, Charlie Perrin style. *What's Charlie Perrin style?* she'd ask. And he'd say, *It's what you're going to be telling your friends about back in . . . wherever you're from.*

A horn blared behind him. He jumped in his seat, then realized he'd slowed down to almost twenty miles an hour. As he accelerated, a blue SUV swung up alongside him. "Learn to drive, asshole!" the man shouted.

Go to hell, Charlie wanted to shout back, and thought about flipping the guy off. Why did people have to be so damn rude? Was it a crime to slow down and check out a girl? Well, sort of. Charlie had no business checking her out, because he already had a great girlfriend—Kate Bryant. Besides, what did he know about seduction? He'd never actually *done it* with anyone. Though he'd come close with Kate. In fact, he had a feeling it might be happening before the end of the summer.

Still, the truth was that he was about as close to being a world-class ladies' man as he was to being a pro basketball star.

But you've got yourself one great set of wheels.

Another horn blared from behind him, this time because he hadn't floored it the instant a traffic light turned green. A few moments later, as he was about to ease into a parking space in front of the Publix grocery store, a rusty green Buick cut right in front of him and stole the spot. He cursed under his breath and ended up driving to the back of the lot before he was able to park the car. Was it him, or were most people just . . . impossible? Sometimes he thought the best plan was to get rich really fast and then buy an island, build a house on it, and issue special passes, *maybe* one a year, to girls who wanted to come and visit. He'd written a composition about that very idea for Mr. Metcalf's philosophy class last year, and after reading it, Mr. Metcalf had approached him with the paper, clucking his tongue the way he did when he was amused. "Charlie, Charlie," he'd said, half smiling. "Nice idea, but you need to read your John Donne. 'No man is an island.'"

"I don't want to *be* an island," Charlie had told him. "I want to *live* on one."

Mr. Metcalf had clucked his tongue again. "I understand that. But people need people, Charlie. You can be as cynical as you like, but you're still going to find that out. It's why we live in societies. There's no way around it: People need people."

Charlie had wanted to tell him he sounded like a corny love song. Metcalf was an oddball. He wore bow ties and shoes with little leather tassels. If Metcalf had his own island, he wouldn't be issuing passes to any *girls*, that was for sure.

Charlie walked across the hot asphalt of the

parking lot, then passed through the automatic doors and into the icy, welcome air of the Publix. He had some serious shopping to do. That morning, before he'd left for work, he'd noticed there was almost no food in the house at all, and he certainly couldn't count on his father to go to the store during the day. In all likelihood, his father hadn't even left the house. He'd practically become a hermit since Charlie's mother had died.

When she first got sick, they explained it to Charlie as if he were a little kid. The red cells were fighting with the white ones over who got to control the blood, and the white cells were winning, but they didn't know how to take care of the blood once they'd won it. "The body is a remarkable machine," one doctor had told him, frowning over the top of a silver clipboard. "We're still learning how to care for it, and there are things we haven't figured out yet." All Charlie knew was that his mother had felt tired for six months, then had been bedridden for six more. She'd always been thin, but she'd grown even thinner, and her hair had turned almost completely white. It wasn't until she went into the hospital that anyone uttered the word *leukemia* in front of him. "Is she going to get better?" Charlie asked his father point-blank one night when they got home from another visit to the hospital.

"We need to take this one day at a time," his father told him.

"But—is she going to get better?"

"She might."

Charlie felt a panic in his chest as if a giant hand were squeezing his ribs. "Well, what if she doesn't?"

"I don't know!" his father snapped. He almost never raised his voice to anyone. "I'm sorry, Charlie. I don't mean to yell at you. I just don't know right now."

"Is she"—the words stuck in Charlie's throat, swelling, threatening to choke him—"is she going to die?"

No, he wanted to hear his father say. *Absolutely not. Get the thought out of your head.* Instead, his father broke down and grabbed Charlie and hugged him. Charlie was already taller than his father. He had to stoop to rest his chin on his father's shoulder, but he wanted his chin there: He wanted to use it like a hook, wanted, suddenly, to hang from and be supported by his father. For what felt like a very long time, the two of them had stood there in the kitchen clutching each other, their bodies shaking as they quietly sobbed.

Not long after that, while she was still in the hospital, Charlie's mother had died.

Things had changed when she'd gotten sick—so much so that you would have thought they couldn't change any more. But once she died, everything changed again. For the past year, every morning when Charlie opened his eyes, he felt like he had to relearn his life, relearn that his mother was dead and that everything was different now.

His father was different, too. Since they'd been on their own, he'd all but stopped going in to work, and he did little more now than sit around the house reading books, mulling over the newspaper, staring at the television for long hours, and taking naps that lasted half a day, sometimes. He was a real estate agent, and a good one. But he hadn't sold a house, or even *tried* to sell one, for nearly a year. In fact, the only thing Charlie could really remember his father *doing* in the past year was taking down all the pictures of Charlie's mother and putting her clothes in the attic. To make matters worse, he'd started drinking in the evenings— something he'd stopped doing entirely, years ago. He drank vodka with orange juice usually, though sometimes he drank wine, sipping it slowly and steadily, like hot tea. He never got angry or violent or anything like that; he just drank until it seemed like someone had kidnapped the brain out of his body. He fell asleep most nights without getting ready for bed. Sometimes he passed out on the couch, sometimes on the living-room recliner, once while he was sitting at the kitchen table. It was a situation Charlie hoped would take care of itself, given enough time. For now, it just meant more responsibility for Charlie.

"Chicken," he mumbled to himself, looking over his list and glancing down into the basket. "Frozen veggies. Yogurt." He'd hurriedly compiled the list on the back of an ATM receipt while eating his lunch that afternoon. His scribble was so chaotic and tiny that he could hardly read it. "Ketchup. Bologna. American cheese. Oh, shit." He'd completely forgotten about cleaning supplies. Both the bathrooms at home needed a good scrubbing, and they were completely out of Comet and Tilex. He shoved the list back into his pocket and hurriedly wheeled the cart back to the cleaning supply aisle.

"Whoa, Perrin, where's the fire?"

Wade Henson was standing at the entrance to the cleaning aisle, blocking Charlie's cart. He was one of those guys who went to the gym but did a half-assed job of it, working their arms and shoulders but never their legs, so they ended up top-heavy and freakish looking. He was wearing a tank top that showed off his bloated shoulders. A faint wisp of a mustache, the same shade of orange as his mullet-cut hair, was sprouting above his upper lip. "Good thing I ran into you. I was going to stop by your house later on—"

"My *house*?" Charlie wouldn't have guessed that Wade even knew where he lived.

"—but I guess I don't have to now." He ran his dull gaze over Charlie and sniffed loudly. "You look pretty skanked out, man."

"I've been working."

"Have you? Derrick will be glad to hear that."

Charlie felt the blood rising in his neck. He had liked Derrick Harding once, but he had never liked

Wade Henson. If Derrick were a ship, Wade would be a barnacle. Charlie suspected that not even Derrick liked Wade but he kept him around because Wade would do anything Derrick said.

A case of Black Label beer dangled from the end of one of Wade's thick arms. He was older than Charlie, but only by three years, Charlie knew, because he'd been a senior at Cernak High School when Charlie was a freshman. *Fake I.D.*, Charlie thought.

"Just tell Derrick—"

"You know what?" Wade said. "Why don't *you* tell him?" He fished his free hand into a pocket of his baggy shorts, brought out a cell phone, and wagged it in the air.

The blood was really pounding in Charlie's ears now. "I don't need to talk him. Just tell him I'll take care of it."

"He knows that." A laugh bubbled out of Wade's mouth like gas. "Question is, when?"

"When I get some money!" Charlie spoke louder than he'd meant to. He glanced around the grocery aisle nervously. In a softer voice, he said, "When I get some money, okay?"

Wade put the phone back into his pocket. "You

crack me up, Perrin. You work more than anybody I know. I mean, you work like a grown-up. Look at you, you even grocery shop like a housewife. You've got to be the most responsible dumb jock on the planet. Where's all your money go?"

It goes, Charlie thought. *Man, does it go.* Car insurance. Gasoline. Upkeep. A new stereo he had no business buying. Not to mention all the dates he'd been going on with Kate.

This was insane. He wasn't going to be pushed around in a grocery store by a parasite like Wade Henson. "That's none of your damn business," he bit out.

The smirk melted off Wade's face and his eyes closed a little, as if Charlie had gone fuzzy. "You're right, Perrin. It's not my business. But it's Derrick's. And he's the one who asked me to check into it."

"I'll call him."

"You ought to."

"I said I'll call him. Whatever it is, I'll take care of it."

Wade nodded his mullet head. He held up his free hand, the fingers and thumb spread wide.

"What's that mean?" Charlie asked.

"Five."

Five what? Five o'clock? Charlie started to shrug, impatient to get away from this jerk ... but then realized what Wade was communicating. It was a sum. The amount he'd stupidly let accumulate with a minus sign in front of it, because for a long time Derrick had been so relaxed about it and hadn't seemed to care at all. Five hundred dollars.

"That's a lot of buzz," Wade said, dropping his hand. "Somebody's got to pay for it. I'm just glad it's not me."

"Why does he need it now, all of a sudden?"

"Electronics. Sound. He's landed a sweet DJ gig up in Jacksonville, but he's got to get the equipment before he can start. So all the unsettled accounts have got to be, you know, settled."

"Well, I'm going to take care of it. Tell Derrick he doesn't have to worry about that."

Wade produced the phone again. Charlie kept his hands gripped around the handle of the shopping cart. Finally Wade sank the phone back into his pocket and said, "See you around, jock."

2.

(I'm not a narc.)

"You want to do it one more time?"

"Yeah!"

"All right—*here we go!*"

There was a heavy rumble, followed by several loud bangs down the hall, then a tremendous crash that shook the walls.

"YAY!"

"You're a regular Dale Earnhardt, Jr., kid."

Sam lifted his head a few inches off his pillow and glared at the door of his room as if trying to blast it with a laser beam. He heard Hannah say, "I love you,

Teddy!" on the other side.

Teddy let out a booming laugh.

Sam groaned and dropped his face back into the pillow. What had he been dreaming? Not one of the flying dreams; those were the best. No, he'd been dreaming about his parents. They were smiling and posing with their arms around each other, in front of some big hole like the Grand Canyon. They were asking Sam to take their picture. But Sam had forgotten to buy film and didn't want them to find out. He'd raised the empty camera and peered nervously through the lens. "Say cheese."

"You two better not break my laundry basket." His mom's voice sounded from the other end of the house.

"Party pooper!"

"Hey, Brenda," Teddy called, "you want me to hang those wall sconces this morning?"

"Oh, that would be great, Teddy."

Yeah, Sam thought, *great*. Now the big ape would be slamming a hammer against the wall for the next two hours. So much for sleeping late. Why couldn't Teddy have a regular job like normal people, instead of one that gave him these giant pockets of free time? He'd been coming over a lot lately—whenever his mom wasn't working at the chamber of commerce. He drank their coffee. He ate their food. He made that annoying, prolonged *Mmmmm* sound whenever he kissed Sam's mom.

Sam had stayed up till almost two A.M. the night before, watching a movie he'd selected from the cable menu only because it had a name that sounded dirty: *The 400 Blows.* It turned out to be old and not dirty at all—except for the part where the boy took off his rain-soaked clothes and slipped into bed naked: For a split second Sam had caught a glimpse of his bare hip, enough to see that the boy *really was* naked. The kid lived in a little apartment where he had no privacy because his family was always hanging over him—they might as well have made that part of the movie about Sam.

As if jumping on this very thought, his little sister swung open the door and walked into his room.

"Hey! Jeez, could you knock?" Sam yanked the sheet up around his waist.

"Don't be a grouch," Hannah said, gazing around

at his posters and at his clothes lying at the foot of the bed as if the place just amazed her, as if she hadn't been in his room a million times before. "Slipped my mind, I guess."

"Well, there's such a thing as *privacy*, and you're violating mine when you come barging in here without knocking."

"Sorry." Hannah continued to snoop her eyes around the room. She was ten, six years younger than Sam, and too curious—too *nosy*—for Sam's taste. She was wearing a ROOF-SMART T-shirt that hung down over her shorts, and her hair was pulled into two ponytails that sprouted out over her ears like crabgrass. "Can I wear your Dolphins cap?"

"No," Sam said.

She pulled the cap off the handle of his closet door and put it on. "Yes, I can. *May* I?"

"*No.*" He reached out and snatched the cap from her head. But then she frowned at him, and he put it back on her and tugged it down over her eyes. "You look like a roadie."

"What's a roadie?"

"Someone who follows rock bands around the

country. Someone so junked out on smack, she can't even remember which band she's traveling with."

"What's smack?" she asked, but she didn't seem to really want to know (and Sam wouldn't have told her anyway). "You're weird." She was slipping a bare foot down into one of his running shoes. "Mom says to come eat breakfast before it's lunchtime."

"I'm not hungry." He was starving. "Hey, don't touch my sunglasses."

Hannah already had them on. She looked at him, wearing his sunglasses, his Dolphins cap, and his running shoes. Her hips started swaying and her hands pawed the air. "I'm *Sam*. I'm *cool*. I'm *Sam-I-am*."

His body was behaving now. He'd slept in his boxer shorts, thankfully, and not in the raw (though he'd thought about it after watching that movie). He shot out his arm like a big hook and dragged her onto the bed. She squealed as he tickled her beneath her arms.

When she was thoroughly conquered, he let her go and sat back against his headboard. "Why are you wearing that dumbass shirt?"

"You owe a quarter to the swearing jar," she told

him, straightening the cap on her head.

"Yeah, I'll be paying that real soon."

Hannah looked down at the shirt and tugged on its hem. "Teddy gave me this."

"He gave me one, too. Know what I did with mine? Cut it up into rags."

"You're so weird," she said. Then she stared at his floor, at the piles of clothes and the scattered CD cases. "You're a slob. Can we call Dad?"

"Why, so you can tell him what a slob I am?"

"No," she said firmly. "I'm not a narc."

She really was a funny little kid, for being a nosy snoop. "We just called him yesterday. He said he was going to call us next time. Friday, I think. Hey, what time is it in London?"

"How should I know?"

"Come on. What did I teach you?"

She rolled her eyes. "Some weird science thing."

"Time zones," he said. "Remember? How Grand-dad is in Nashville, and he's an hour behind us?"

"I *know,*" she groaned.

"Well, people in London are five hours ahead. We're here"—he made a fist and pointed to his thumb knuckle—"and Dad is . . . here." He pointed to the knuckle of his third finger. "It's ten o'clock in St. Augustine, so what time is it in London?"

"Fifteen o'clock," she said, screwing her face up like a moron.

"You're brilliant," Sam said. "I'll bet you're just oozing brilliance all over the inside of my cap." He got out of bed, grabbed a T-shirt from the floor, and pulled it on. From another pile, he found a pair of cutoff shorts and climbed into them. "Be right back, Jack."

As he crossed the hall to the bathroom, he heard voices coming from the front of the house. More conversation about wall sconces. When he came back into his room, Hannah was lying down flat on her back across the foot of his bed, her head hanging over the side. Looking at him upside down, through his sunglasses, she said, "Dad's with his friend, isn't he?"

"Yeah."

Hannah huffed. She rolled over. "I wish he'd come home."

"He'll be home in, like, three weeks."

"I mean *home*," she said.

He knew what she meant, of course. It had been almost a year since their parents had gotten separated. There'd been a lot of arguments leading up to the event, most of them behind closed doors—that awful, muffled sound of angry adults trying not to be heard. Then there were a few very loud arguments, which Sam had drowned out with his headphones. But even though the fighting went on for a few weeks, he was still shocked when his parents sat him and Hannah down and told them the news: Their dad was going to move out of the house. There'd been a thousand questions, most of them from Hannah ("For how long?" and "How come you don't just stop fighting?" and, over and over and over again, "Why?"), and none of the answers had been very specific. "It's for the best," they both said. But how could that make any sense? How was it for the best when their dad was moving up to Ponte Vedra Beach?

They went to his new house almost every weekend, either dropped off by his mom or picked up by his dad—though they never spent the night. His dad's new house was larger and nicer than theirs. It had a pool, and Sam and Hannah kept swimsuits there so they could go swimming when they went over. The house was owned by a man named David, who shared the living space.

His dad was an architect who sometimes wrote textbooks, and he was working on a new one now. David was some sort of financial consultant.

David was nice, and funny, and maybe a little older than Sam's dad. Hannah was crazy about him—though she tended to toss affection around like confetti, Sam thought, remembering the comment he'd heard her make that morning: "I love you, Teddy." Ugh! Sam liked David, too. He was always relaxed. Sam's dad even seemed relaxed—for the first time in Sam couldn't remember how long. He seemed *happy*. Sam had been glad for him, but he hadn't quite understood. Was a new friend and a bigger house enough to turn someone around, make him a happy, smiling person? Was it enough to make him want to start a whole new life?

"You know your mother and I still care about each other a great deal," his dad had told him once, when they were alone in the kitchen.

"But you don't want to live together?"

"That's right. On a certain level, we just didn't get along. It happens with people, and the best thing they can do is be honest with each other about how they feel; otherwise, they just stay unhappy. But it doesn't mean we're not still a family. We are. Always remember that."

"But we're not," Sam said, confused. "You and Mom don't even like talking to each other on the phone."

"Well, people fight, Sam. Sometimes the fight gets so big that you can't pretend it's not there anymore, you know what I mean? I still care about your mother, and I want you to know that I'm always there for you. And for Hannah, too. We're still a family."

Whatever, Sam had wanted to say, because it still didn't make sense to him.

Then, several months ago, it all became clear— sort of. Sam and Hannah had come over for a cookout by the pool. Hannah was practicing cannonballs, and Sam dried off and went into the house to use the bathroom. As he turned into the hall, he saw

David sitting at the desk in his bedroom, staring at the computer. "This is great!" David said. "Thank you! It's twice as fast now. You must have cleaned out a lot of junk." Then Sam's dad appeared behind David, put his hands on David's shoulders, and leaned over. He looked at the computer screen for a moment, then kissed the side of David's neck and said, "You're welcome."

Sam had ducked into the bathroom and quietly closed the door. He stared at himself in the large mirror behind the sink, utterly confused. His dad didn't seem gay. Neither did David. And if they *were* gay, then why would his dad have married his mom in the first place? Was this something his dad had just recently figured out? Sam couldn't wrap his brain around it. His mother had wrapped *her* brain around it, that was for sure. It must have been what all those fights were about, back when his dad still lived with them.

Hannah, Sam was certain, had no idea. She was such a blabbermouth that she would have said something to him by now.

It was almost too crazy to think about—except that, in a way, Sam had *always* thought about two guys together that way; he'd been imagining what it would be like to kiss and touch another boy since he was, what, ten? He'd tried to make himself *not* imagine it, but that had proved impossible. And he'd spent a lot of time worrying about how people might react if they found out about him. Especially his family.

Now, knowing what his parents had gone through and how it had split them apart, his situation only seemed worse. It was like his dad had done something wrong, and now Sam wanted to venture into that same territory, which would only upset everyone, and everything, all over again. Granted, there was gay stuff all over the place—in the news, on TV shows, in the movies—but still, for the most part, people he knew just made fun of it. He'd gone to a large birthday party last spring for Mike Chupnik, the sportswriter on the school newspaper staff, and they'd had *Dude, Where's My Car?* playing on the television. No one was paying much attention to the movie, but then right in the middle of it, Ashton Kutcher and Seann William Scott leaned into each other and, out of the blue, shared a serious lip-lock. While Sam was absorbed by the sight, one of the other guys in the living room started howling and making gross-out noises. "I hate this part!" someone else yelled. "It makes me want to puke!" Then Mike, who'd just opened Sam's present, said, "Hey, who invited the fags?"—cracking up everyone in the room but Sam.

How would people react if they knew that not only was Sam Findley's dad a full-fledged homo, but that Sam himself was a homo in the making? They'd probably say his dad had caused it, which was totally ridiculous. They'd probably even make sick jokes about his dad messing around with him. For all Sam knew, his mother might even think something like that. She didn't seem to mind it when Teddy made stupid, homophobic remarks.

"It's not so bad," he told Hannah now, wanting to make her feel better and wanting to change the topic. "Just think of it like Dad lives up the road. That's all. He's just right up the road."

"Why's he in London, anyway?"

"Because of David's job," Sam said, and instantly wished he hadn't. He knew it would only prompt another question from his little sister.

"Why can't just David be there?"

"Because Dad wants to be there to research his

architecture book. He told you that."

"What's wrong with the buildings here?"

"I don't know," Sam snapped. He really wanted to change the subject now and was relieved to see Jasbo waddle into the room. "Wow, is Jasbo fatter than he was yesterday?"

Hannah jumped off the bed and squatted down, holding her arms out to the copper-colored dachshund. "He's fat as a piglet. Come here, Jasbo. Bring your fat butt over here." Jasbo made his way across the carpet and lowered his head, allowing Hannah to scratch his neck. "You're a good old fat dog, aren't you?"

"Has he eaten breakfast?"

"He's been eating all morning! He ate half my egg."

"Well, let's go feed him half of mine," Sam said, and ushered his sister out of the room. The dog waddled after them.

3.

Things would make more sense if Charlie woke up one day to find that someone had actually cloned him when he was a baby, and that all along there had been five of him. It would explain how one of the Charlie Perrins was just this normal, happy-go-lucky guy with a girlfriend and a car and a year left to go in high school. And how another Charlie Perrin was a slacker who walked around feeling sad whenever any thought of his mother entered his mind, which was about a million times a day. And how the third

Charlie Perrin was able to think of his future and imagine grand success on a pro ball team, while the fourth had already concluded that he was a loser and a daydreamer. And then there was the fifth Charlie Perrin, who seemed to have never even met the other four, and who liked closing out the entire world and getting high.

He'd smoked pot for the first time almost a year ago, a few weeks after his mother died. A couple of teammates—Troy and Taylor Sullivan, twins who were good players but not exactly his friends—had invited him over after the team had won an afternoon game against Ocala. Charlie had played well, scoring twenty-five points. With the brothers, in the rec room of their large house, he ate hot dogs and watched a movie and played a half dozen games of Splinter Cell. Then Taylor put on some music and closed the blinds.

"Hey," Troy said, dropping down next to Charlie where he sat cross-legged in front of their giant television, "good game today."

"Really good game," Taylor said from the stereo. "You were electric."

"Thanks." Charlie felt himself nod. "You guys were great, too."

"Just doing our jobs," Troy said. "So, hey. You been doing okay?"

"Fine," Charlie said. He was still looking at the TV screen but felt the twins' gaze from either side. He set down the joystick. "You?"

"Sorry to hear about your mom dying and all," Taylor blurted out.

Troy shot his brother a look. "Yeah. Sorry about that. That really sucks."

Charlie had no idea what to say. Yes, it sucked? Thank you?

"Our mom," Troy said, "you know, *her* mom died when she was really young—when *our* mom was really young—and she told us it was awful, and that it, it must be really rough on you."

So that was why they'd asked him over all of a sudden, having never talked to him off the basketball court before. Their own mother had put them up to it. *You two ought to ask that poor Perrin boy over to the house. He could probably use some cheering up.* Charlie felt the hot dogs he'd eaten start to churn in his stomach. He didn't really want to be in the Sullivan house any longer but didn't know how to just leave, since he was dependent on Mrs. Sullivan for a ride home.

Fortunately, both Troy and Taylor seemed more than ready to move on from the topic of his mother, now that it had been officially acknowledged. Taylor stepped away from the stereo and reached up high on the DVD shelf for a small wooden box. He lifted the lid and took out a twisted cigarette. "Want to get high?"

"Yeppers," Troy said.

Charlie looked from one brother to the other. Were they serious? He tried to sound casual. "What about your parents?"

"They *never* come in here. The only person in here besides us is the cleaning lady."

Taylor chuckled. "And she wouldn't say a word, because she doesn't want to get deported."

Charlie felt himself shrug. He nodded.

The three of them shared the joint, which made Charlie cough, but almost immediately he felt more comfortable in the twins' rec room. They laughed at how red his eyes looked, though their eyes looked red, too. The music, whatever it was, started to sound incredibly great.

"Are there any more hot dogs?" Charlie asked.

"Why? You hungry?"

"Yeah. I don't why, though. I just ate."

Troy and Taylor started laughing again. Charlie started laughing, too. "You're *stoned*," one of them said, and the other one said, "You. Are. Stoned."

This seemed enormously funny, and the three of them laughed for what felt like half an hour.

Finally Troy cleared his throat and said, "You know, you're a cool guy."

"Thanks," Charlie said, wiping his eyes with his fingers.

"He is," Taylor said. "You are. When our dad, you know, when we told him we wanted to try out for the basketball team, he started bitching about how he never should have put that hoop in the driveway. 'You boys join the basketball team, you're going to be hanging out with nothing but blacks.'"

Troy cracked up at his brother's impression of their father. "That's *exactly* what he said!"

"And we were like, I don't think so. White guys play basketball, too. Of course, he was kind of right. I mean, there *are* a lot of black guys on the team this year."

"More than a lot," Troy said.

"And it's not so great wondering if you're gonna get, you know, mugged in the middle of a game," Taylor said.

Charlie had been laughing all through this. He stopped. "Huh?"

Taylor shrugged. "I know it's a cliché, but clichés are based on truth, after all."

Charlie cleared his throat. He wiped his eyes again. "Wow," he said. "You guys really *are* snobs."

The amusement drained out of both brothers' faces simultaneously. "We're not snobs," one them said.

"Well, okay. Racist."

"We're not *racist*," the other one bit out, sounding shocked. "We're *real*."

"Well, when you say . . . when you say . . ." Charlie couldn't figure out how to vocalize what he was thinking. Suddenly he realized he didn't have to. "Wow. I'm feeling pretty good."

"Are you?"

"Yeah. The only thing is . . ." He glanced at the brothers, squinting. "I see two of you." This cracked him up until he was practically folded over with laughter. The twins looked bemused; they'd probably heard this joke before. "Where do you guys get this stuff?" Charlie asked.

"The buzz?" one of them asked—was it Taylor or Troy? Who cared?—and then made a thumbs-up with one hand. "Our Dr. Feelgood goes by the name of Derrick Harding."

"Derrick Harding," Charlie repeated, trying to place the name. "Graduated last year? Kicked out of student government?"

"The very same," one of the twins said. "We should give you his number."

And they did. Charlie never hung out with the twins again after that night. He never wanted to. But a week later he called the number they'd given him. Derrick remembered him from high school. He invited Charlie over to his apartment, got him stoned, sent him home with a sandwich Baggie of pot. Derrick was as friendly as could be. He was funny and easy to be around and generous: He always sent Charlie home with a bag, which he told Charlie not to worry about paying for. "Later," was his famous line. "You can pay me later."

A year had passed like smoke in a breeze. Suddenly, later was now.

When Charlie got home from the grocery store, his father was at the kitchen table with the newspaper spilled out in front of him, several pieces of it on the floor next to his feet. Without looking up, he said, "There's Charlie."

A glass of weak-looking orange juice sat next to his elbow.

"Hi, Dad." Charlie set the grocery bags on the counter. "I picked up some food on the way home."

"Oh—thank you."

As he unpacked the bags, Charlie listened to the newspaper pages turning, as slowly and regularly as sedated breathing. His father reached the end of the section, then turned the paper over and started paging through it again. He was dressed in pajama pants and a white T-shirt, but he had on his bedroom slippers. Sometimes he spent entire days in his pajamas.

"I started reglazing the windows of the Danforth house today," Charlie said. "It's pretty cool, because I'm replacing all the cracked windowpanes, too, and the only way to get them out is to smash them with a hammer."

His father didn't look up from the paper. It was as if he hadn't heard a word Charlie had said. Charlie raised his voice a notch and asked, "What did you do today, Dad?" He already knew the answer.

"Me? I kept pretty busy." His father cleared his throat and squinted at an article.

"Did you go anywhere?"

"Why do you always ask me that?"

Charlie shrugged. "Just curious."

"I went downtown to the office, took a look at some new listings."

"How was that?"

His father cleared his throat again. "Not a lot going on this time of year. Fall's better. Less rental action, more buying."

Charlie didn't believe him. In fact, he didn't think his father had left the house in days. "Did you eat lunch out?" he asked, trying to sound casual.

"Me?" *Who else?* "No. I ate here."

Charlie didn't believe this, either. There hadn't been anything to eat in the house, except maybe cornflakes. "You need to eat, Dad."

"I ate," he said to the paper. "Don't harass me, son."

"Well, I've got to get cleaned up. Then I'll make us some spaghetti, okay?"

There was such a long stretch of silence, Charlie started to wonder if he'd been heard. Then, as if he didn't even know what they were talking about, his father said, "Okay, Charlie."

He showered, spending a long time under the spray with his eyes closed, the warm water batting against his forehead. *I wish, I wish, I wish*, he thought. *I wish Mom was here. She'd put Dad back on track.* Though that didn't really make any sense, because his father wouldn't be in the shape he was in if his mother hadn't died. *I wish I'd spent more time on the court this summer. I wish I'd never laid eyes on Derrick Harding. Why in the hell did I ever get involved with that guy?*

Of course he knew why. Despite his ability to play a pretty good game, he didn't fit in with the jocks—at least, not with those guys who talked about nothing but sports and walked around like they held the deed to the school in their hand. And since his mother had died, he wasn't exactly in the mood to meet new people. He had a—what was the word? He'd learned it in English this past year. *Dearth*. He had a *dearth* of friends. Guys just to hang out with. Not that he wanted an entourage. In fact, one good friend—a best friend, someone he could really talk to—would probably have been enough to keep him from sucking up to a creep like Derrick Harding.

Someone like Sam Findley.

But that friendship was over. Charlie didn't even know why. He and Sam had been best friends since they were nine, and then one day their friendship had just . . . stopped. Sam was the one who had ended it, and he'd never explained why. They both lived in the same neighborhood, they went to the same school, but for over a year now, since before Charlie's mother first got sick, they hadn't spoken a word to each other.

Charlie finished showering and pulled on a T-shirt and a pair of basketball shorts. As he stood in the kitchen boiling the spaghetti, he thought about going down to the court at the end of their neighborhood and shooting some baskets. But his father went back to vodka and orange juice before they started eating, and by the time Charlie was loading the dishwasher, he'd downed at least three. He started making little remarks to the news program on TV ("You think so?" "I doubt it!" "Oh, come on, where's the hard evidence for *that*?"), and Charlie got so irritated that he lost his energy and just retreated to his room.

He'd earned a little unwinding time, hadn't he? He'd worked for eight hours, dealt with Wade, brought home the bacon—more than enough crap for one day. He had his unwinding routine perfected: He cranked open his window, set the little gray fan on the sill, then dug his pipe and lighter and film container of pot from the bottom drawer of his nightstand. Crouching in front of the fan, he lit up and puffed, exhaling smoke that was immediately sucked outside.

Not long after that, he was lying flat on his bed,

listening to music and thinking about the girl he'd seen coming out of Gatorland. He rolled over onto his hand.

Then he remembered Kate: He was supposed to have called her an hour ago. He scrambled for the phone on his nightstand and dialed.

"Hello?"

"Hi," he said. "It's me."

"I thought you were going to call earlier than this."

"Sorry. My dad made me do all this stuff around the house as soon as I got home." He'd never told Kate about how his father had started drinking again since his mom died (not that she knew he'd had a problem in the first place). "I just completely lost track of time. What are you up to?"

"I had this enormous fight with my mom. She doesn't want me borrowing the car anymore because, get this, she says I got it *too dirty* the last time I used it. Remember that big rainstorm a couple of weeks ago? She said I splashed mud all over the fenders. I said, hey, did I make the storm? Blame God. Well, that *really* got her mad. You would have thought I'd torn a page out of the Bible."

Kate was a force of nature. She was strong willed, and spoke her mind, and didn't put up with any bull from anyone. It was what had first attracted Charlie to her back when they'd had sociology class together and she'd spoken up so freely about stereotypes and "looks-ism" (Charlie still wasn't sure what "looks-ism" was, but he liked hearing Kate rail against it). And she wasn't only smart, she was the hottest girl in the school, as far as he was concerned. Mellowing into the thought of her, he said simply, "You're great."

"For what, fighting with my mom?"

"I mean it. You're really just . . . great."

"Um, thanks. You sound kind of out of it. You're not high, are you?"

"No," he lied. She knew he'd smoked pot in the past, and she didn't like it. In fact, they'd argued about it just a few weeks ago. She had this whole philosophy about how a person who took mind-altering drugs was basically just an escape artist who was dodging the real issues in his life. In a way, Charlie agreed with her. But didn't people need to dodge stuff now and then? In the end, he'd decided it was easier to lie to her than to argue; she was much

more articulate than he was, and he could never keep up. "I'm just beat. I worked on the Danforth house all day. They don't even have the power turned on, so I can't use the AC. It wipes me out."

"Charlie Horse is tired," she said.

He felt relieved. She only called him Charlie Horse when she was feeling affectionate. "Not too tired to pick up where we left off last Saturday," he said, grinning.

"I'll bet."

"You were pretty amazing."

"You weren't so bad yourself. Hey, do you want to go to the beach this week? During the daytime, like regular people?"

"You got it. I'm flexible with my work hours. The Danforths haven't even moved into the place yet. When do you want to go?"

"How about Thursday?"

"I'm aallll yours."

"Good. You really sound out of it. You should go to sleep."

"I'm going to," he said. "I'm giving you a big, long good-night kiss."

43

"Yeah, yeah, *smooch*," she said. "Go to sleep, and call me tomorrow. If I can't use my mom's car, I may need you to drive me to the mall after dinner."

"I am your chariot," he said.

"You're my Charlie Horse."

"I'm your stud."

"Go to *bed*."

After they hung up, he rolled over onto his hand again. But instead of feeling charged up about his conversation with Kate, he only felt tired, and before long he dozed off.

4.

(We don't say that word.)

Teddy was standing on the sofa with his shoes on, hefting a power drill. "Chowderhead!" he said loudly when he saw Sam emerge from the back of the house. "Where've you been?"

"Trying to sleep. Until a laundry basket crashed into my door."

"You should have seen Big'un here fly!"

Chowderhead. Big'un. Teddy had a knack for getting on Sam's nerves. He was slightly pear shaped, and his weight was stabbing his shoes down into the sofa cushions. Sam's mom would have had a fit if she saw Sam or Hannah doing that. But chunky, clunky, loudmouthed Teddy walked on water.

"You and Crabcake going to help me hang some wall sconces?"

Hannah giggled, which only irritated Sam more. "Her name's Hannah," he said. "And I've got stuff to do."

"Sam," his mother called out sharply. She was in the kitchen, leaning back from the sink to put Sam in her sight line. "What have I told you about being rude?"

"Sorry," Sam said, looking away from both his mom and Teddy, glancing at Hannah, who was perched on the arm of the sofa.

"I'm going to give you stuff to do if you don't straighten up, young man."

"I said sorry."

Teddy either didn't notice or didn't care when Sam got smart with him. He raised the drill and squeezed the trigger, tearing into the wall.

Sam poured himself a glass of juice. He took the scrambled egg his mom had cooked him and made a sandwich with toast and a few pieces of bacon.

Jasbo watched him. Sam tossed out a sliver of egg, and the dachshund caught it in midair. His mother was loading the dishwasher. Her blond hair, the exact same shade as Sam's and Hannah's, was pulled back into a ponytail. She'd started wearing it that way when Teddy came into the picture. That was also about the time she'd decided that the entire look of the house had to change, as if leaving it the way it was when his father had lived here was unthinkable. What did they need with wall sconces? She glanced at him, then folded her arms over her stomach and nodded toward his plate. "Put that in the dishwasher when you're through eating."

"Affirmative, captain."

"Tell me something, because I really want to know. I'm going to mark it on my calendar. When are you going to snap out of this attitude?" she asked.

Sam shrugged and said through a mouthful, "What are you talking about? I'm just standing here eating an egg."

"The boy needs his protein!" Teddy called from the living room, over the shriek of the drill. "Got to put some meat on those bones. He's going to need 'em to wax that new shed to keep it from rusting."

Sam rolled his eyes.

"*That's* what I'm talking about," his mother said softly, so that only Sam could hear. "I don't want to see you roll your eyes or hear that sarcastic tone in your voice. We've talked about this."

Sam swallowed, then reached for the juice glass. "Affirmative. No more eye rolling."

"Darn it!" Teddy announced to the wall. "Brenda, do you have any screw anchors?"

"I don't think so. What are they?"

"Those little plastic jobbers that hold the screws into the drywall. I'll bet the guy who invented those is a millionaire. Probably a Japanese."

"I don't think we have any."

"Darn it. Who wants to go to the hardware store?"

"Me!" Hannah shouted.

What a pushover, Sam thought. You'd think the hardware store was Disney World.

Teddy blew drywall dust off the drill bit and said, "Sam?"

"I'm going running," Sam said. "Thanks, though."

He set his plate down, leaned forward, and kissed his mom's cheek. "See?" he whispered. "I'm a model of politeness."

This time she was the one who rolled her eyes. Sam headed off toward his room.

His ancient Discman wasn't working. He put new batteries in it, but it was still dead. That's what he got for buying a cheap model he'd never heard of. He wanted to get away from the house before Teddy and Hannah came out to leave for the hardware store, so he didn't stretch for nearly as long as he normally would have. For the first ten minutes, he suffered. But eventually the muscles in his legs started to heat up and feel as if they were moving on their own. He left the neighborhood and made his way out to San Marco Avenue, where he ran against traffic. He passed the neon signs for the Fountain of Youth and the Ripley Museum. (It was hard to believe people actually paid to see that stuff. Why didn't they just throw their money into the street? He pictured the Believe It or Not headline for the story: *St. Augustine tourists throw dollars into the street for amusement*—

*AND LOCAL BOY RUNS AWAY WITH THEIR
MONEY!)*

San Marco Avenue took him down to the Bridge
of Lions. The water was choppy and dotted with
bobbing fishing boats, and the wind, once he was
out on the bridge, was crazy. But Sam liked the feel
of it: shoving into his chest, like a giant hand, then
not there at all, then smacking into his back and
driving him forward. He crossed over onto Anastasia
Island. From there, he left the main road and followed a path through the palmetto scrub, out to the
beach at the island's northern tip. Damp sand—a few
feet away from the tide line—was his favorite running surface. Just enough cushion. Just enough resist-
ance. He was flying now, kicking chunks of sand up
behind him and sending gangs of seagulls flapping
out over the water. He was drenched in sweat, his
mind engaged only with his speed, his form, and
dodging the occasional beached jellyfish.

But soon his shins started to feel like burning
sticks of wood. He turned around, finally, and headed
back, but he was far from home when he had to slow
down and eventually surrender to walking.

When he got back to his house, Teddy's car was gone. He opened the front door and felt the air conditioning seal onto his damp skin.

The phone rang and his mom answered it.

"Hello? . . . Oh, hi, Melissa! Are you ready for the new school year? . . . Mm-hmm . . . And what about colleges, have you started looking into those? . . . That's good. . . . It's never too early to start. . . . Okay . . . Yes, I think I just heard him come in. Sam, is that you?"

He stepped into the living room, still breathing heavily, and nodded.

"Here he is, Melissa. Say hi to your mother for me, all right?" She handed the phone over.

"Hey, Melissa-monster. What's up?"

"I'm so depressed!" Melissa said into his ear. "I can't even tell you."

"Tell me," he said, waving his mom away. She winked at him and returned to the sofa, where she'd been leafing through a book of wallpaper samples.

"Oh, you know. Why get out of bed, have they blown the world up yet, I'm a cow. The usual. What's going on with you?"

"Just got back from running."

"You really ought to give that one up. You're a journalist, not a jock."

"Screw you," Sam said, and mimed a remorseful face when his mother looked up at him.

"Not in this lifetime. Do you want to go with me to the Pistol Museum tomorrow?"

"Why do you want to go *there*?"

"I talked to the curator on the phone today. He's going to let me take some pictures."

"And what are you going to do with them? Decorate your room?"

"Very funny. I want to do a series of photos about handgun legislation for the fall art fair. The curator doesn't know that, but I don't think he'd care; he sounded about a hundred years old. Anyway, I want to do a kind of eerie gun montage, then get some shots of the jail, and maybe ride out to the Old Spanish Cemetery."

"Sounds like an uplifting afternoon. I can't go, though. I'm working straight through Sunday."

"Yuck," Melissa said. "How much frozen yogurt can people eat?"

"More than you want to know. Somebody's got

to staff the counter. Shapiro—that whiny jerk who usually works weekends? I'm covering for him. Can we do it on Sunday?"

"It's got to be tomorrow afternoon, because they're closing the museum to have the carpets steamed, and the old guy said I could come in before they start."

"Sorry."

"Well, you're still coming over on Monday to watch *The Poseidon Adventure*, right?"

"Absolutely. It's a date," he said—and was immediately sorry he'd chosen the word *date*. His mom raised her head again and smiled at him.

"Okay, I'd better go. I have a yoga class. I'm going to slash if I don't center myself."

"Don't let your karma run over your dogma."

"See, that's how much of a jock you're not. You don't even know what yoga is, and it's the least sporty of sports."

They said good-bye and hung up.

His mom was watching him. "So," she said after a moment, a hesitant smile forming on her lips, "you have a date with Melissa?"

"Just to watch a movie next week at her place. She's been having a classic disaster film festival all summer. *Earthquake, Hurricane, Virus*, a bunch of other stuff I've never even heard of."

"Melissa's a nice girl."

"I guess."

"Is she dating anyone?"

Sam shrugged. "I don't think so. She's kind of on the morbid side, not exactly a romantic."

"I just think she's a nice girl. She told me she's going to apply to the University of Florida because they have a good photography program."

"Yeah, she's mentioned that to me about a hundred times."

"Well, what schools are you considering?"

"Cernak High," he said, then whistled and glanced off to the side as if the point was obvious.

"I'm talking about a year from now, smart aleck. Before you know it, all your friends will be accepted *some*where, and you'll wish you'd given it some thought."

Of course Sam had already started thinking about college. But it irked him that his mom just assumed he didn't care, that she was butting in and trying to control the situation. "I'm not even a senior yet."

"You'll be one in about three weeks. Believe me,

time just flies. What do you think about the University of Florida?"

"I think . . . it's in Gainesville."

"What do you think of it as a *school*?" she emphasized.

"As a school, I think it's in Gainesville. As a concept—"

"*Attitude,*" she reminded him. "Their journalism program is supposed to be good. You're still interested in that, aren't you? You're going to be the editor of the school paper this year; that's the kind of thing that can help you get scholarship money."

"Huh," Sam said, as if he'd never heard of scholarships before.

"It might be worth looking into. What about Charlie?"

Sam blinked. "Charlie *Perrin*? What about him?"

"I'm just wondering what schools he's thinking about. He plays football, right?"

"Basketball. But Charlie and I haven't hung out in over a year."

"There used to be that little group of you that I really liked. You and Charlie and Rudy Walters, and who was that boy who moved to Oregon?"

"No idea."

"Don't be difficult. His name was Loren something." She shook her head. "That was such a terrible thing, when Charlie's mother passed away. Just awful. She went so quickly."

Sam didn't say anything. He'd wanted to call Charlie when he'd heard, but hadn't been able to bring himself to do it.

"Is he doing okay, since then?"

"No idea."

"Does he have a girlfriend? Mrs. Morrow up the street said he was dating that girl Kate Bryant, the one who got that junior spirit trophy at the awards ceremony last year."

"Mom, I *don't know*."

"Well, when did you two stop being friends? After his mother died?"

"No, it was before that."

"And you *never* talk to him? I'm sure he could use a friend. I mean, really, Sam, the Perrins live just three streets over." Sam tilted his head back and closed his eyes. "All right, never mind," she said. "But what happened, anyway? You two were so close. For years. Friendships don't just end all of a sudden."

"This one did."

"Don't tell me if you don't want to, but it's a shame. He's a nice boy."

Sam already knew this. He missed having Charlie as a friend. But he had to accept the situation for what it was. There was no way around it. "Can I . . . keep walking down the hall now? You know, to my room?"

She exhaled. "Go. Just don't forget about the shed."

"What about it?" Suddenly Sam remembered. He felt his energy drain down his legs and into his shoes.

"You're going to wax it this afternoon. That's what we agreed on."

Sam groaned. "It's my day off. I'm not supposed to do *anything*." She tilted her head toward him. "Why can't Teddy do it? He's the one who built the stupid thing. We don't even need it. It's just killing grass."

"Speaking of grass," his mom said, "Teddy mowed it before he put up the shed. Remember? That was very nice of him, and it's one less thing you have to do, so I expect you to stick to what we agreed on and wax the shed. This afternoon."

"Does Teddy live here now, or what?"

"Sam! Would you stop being so difficult?"

"Does he? I'm only asking because he's here all the time."

"He's here as much as I want him to be, young man. And if you don't shape up, you're going to spend the rest of the summer in your room."

Then I won't be able to wax the shed, Sam thought. He retreated down the hall.

She had everything fixed a certain way in her mind. Sam was supposed to be dating Melissa. He and Charlie were supposed to still be best friends. They were all—including Charlie—supposed to dance off to U of F together and live happily ever after. Why didn't she just attach marionette strings to everybody's limbs and put on a show called *Sam's Mom Rules the World*?

He stood on a stepladder in the backyard, spreading gobs of Turtle Wax across the aluminum roof of the shed. He'd taken off his damp shirt, and the gnats had set in. He'd been smacking them when they lit on his chest, and he felt like he had as much wax on him as on the shed. What did his mother see in Teddy? The big ape was at their house for hours every day, yammering on about politics, and sports, and "the immigrants," and "the terrorist-sympathizers" (his term for anyone protesting the war). He talked with his mouth full. And he sat at *the head of the table.* Wasn't that supposed to be Sam's spot, if his dad wasn't going to be there? His dad would never have asked him to do anything as stupid as wax a toolshed they didn't even need. Sam wanted to call London, get his dad on the phone, tell him who was sitting in his chair . . . only he didn't know if his father even cared anymore. It wasn't like he'd been kicked out of the house; he'd chosen to go and live an entirely different life.

At least Teddy hadn't been spending the night at their house. That would be too much to stomach.

Sam gripped the damp rag, dragged it fiercely across the shed, and caught the side of his thumb on a bolt. "Ow!" he yelled. "Shit! Shit, shit, shit!" He threw the rag toward the fence and sucked on his thumb. It wasn't bleeding, but it hurt like hell.

That evening, he asked his mom if they could eat on TV trays, in front of the television. *"No,"* she said firmly. "Any more questions?" Then she handed him the silverware and told him to set the table.

From the head of the table, Teddy dominated the conversation, churning through another stupid sociopolitical lecture and cracking jokes that made his mom smile and made Hannah practically convulse. "I'm telling you, the good folks down at Ex-Lax don't make a chocolate patty big enough for the U.S. government. I don't care which party's in charge, they still can't get a darn thing *done*. It's like one big digestive track that can't . . . poo." He winked at Hannah. She dribbled milk down her chin. "Roof-Smart's not much better. It's just like a little version of the government—lots of backstabbing and lying and what have you. They'd get a heck of a lot more contracts if they listened to me. But they never will. Because the district manager's a knothead who doesn't know one thing about marketing, and the assistant district manager's a bozo fairy who flits around like Tinker Bell, asking you how your *day* is going instead of getting down to the nitty-gritty—"

"I thought we weren't supposed to say *fairy*," Sam interrupted, looking at his mom.

She glanced down at her plate. She wiped her napkin over her lips.

"Why?" Hannah asked.

Sam waited for his mother to answer her. When she didn't, he said, "Because it's one of those words Mom told us not to say. Remember?" He turned to his mother. "I had to write an essay on prejudice, and you helped me look up examples—"

"I remember," his mom said over her napkin.

Sam looked toward the head of the table, into Teddy's eyes. "So we don't say that word."

"Hey, fine with me," Teddy said, chuckling around a mouthful of chicken. "I don't ever have to say *fairy* again. You know Spanish? How about *mariposa*? The Mexicans in the tile department say it all the time. It means butterfly. I'm telling you, this guy really does flit around the office like a butterfly."

Sam looked at his mom again. *Say something to him*, he thought. *Tell him to shut his stupid mouth*. But she only said, "I'm not big on politics at the dinner table."

5.

(Sue me.)

Charlie sprinted from the baseline to the free-throw line and back. From the baseline to half-court and back. From one baseline to the other, and back again—the whole length of the court twice. It was a quick way to get the blood flowing, to get his body warmed up like he would for a game. Not so easy, because the "court" in the small park at the back of the neighborhood was really just a slab of faded asphalt with a rusty hoop at either end, and over the years the painted lines had been sun bleached and trampled by sneakers until they were almost invisible. Also not easy because this one set of line drills had him folded over, hands on his knees, winded. *Perrin!* Coach Bobbit would have screamed. *Get your mind off your dick and get the lead out, son!* But this was just Charlie, alone, come to shoot some hoops. He had only himself to do the yelling. *Up, loser*, he thought. *Another set gonna kill you?* He assumed the position at the baseline and started running all over again.

What about a third set? Is that *gonna kill you?*

A minute later he had his answer: Yes, a third set of line drills would put him in his grave. Breathing heavily, he picked up his ball from the edge of the court and tossed it back and forth between his hands. He ran forward, dribbled, and banked a shot through the hoop. A little on the sloppy side. Too much rattle in the rim. He retrieved the ball and repeated the shot several times, then moved back to half-court and stared furiously at the hoop as he smacked the ball against the asphalt. He ran, dribbling, dodging imaginary opponents. He approached the hoop again. *Perrin curls around the screen, sets himself, and drops a three. Look at him! Shoulders set, great rotation,* swish!

He caught the ball and repeated the shot. Then went at it again.

You'll notice he's got his Air Perrins on—an excellent shoe that's selling all over the country—and there he goes again! This guy really is a master of form. . . .

Clank! Brick shot. The ball missed the rim entirely, got away from him, and bounced across the court until it rolled to a stop under a park bench. *You suck, Perrin*, he told himself. *You've lost your edge. You didn't practice enough this summer.*

Frustrated, he kept himself in constant motion for the next minute, going for fairly easy shots and making each one, seven in a row. "That's better," he said aloud, spinning the ball between the two webs of his hands. He moved into position for a free throw. *Nothing but net*, he thought. *Nothing . . . but . . . net.*

The ball dropped straight through the hoop.

Suddenly he was thinking about Sam. Two summers ago, he and Sam had stood side by side on this same court, in this same heat, and Charlie had tried to teach Sam how to free throw. Sam had been lousy. It became funny after a while; in fact, they were laughing their asses off, because Sam seemed absolutely incapable of judging the distance between himself and the hoop. He watched Charlie intently, nodded at Charlie's instructions, and each time he was handed the ball, he'd just launch the thing into the air as if it were burning his hands, and it would fall short. "You're not even trying," Charlie told him.

"That's just it!" Sam said, laughing. "I *am* trying! That's how pathetic it is!"

"All right, look." Charlie handed him the ball and stood directly behind him. "Here's you. Here's the ball." He reached around either side and raised Sam's elbows until Sam was holding the ball just under his own nose. "There's the hoop."

"Hi, hoop," Sam said.

"*Visualize,*" Charlie told him. "You have to focus your mind and *see* this happening. You're gonna shoot the ball, it's gonna fly straight from your hands to that hoop, and it's gonna drop right in. Whoosh. Nothing but net. You got it? *Visualize.*"

He heard Sam's breathing, felt a slight tremble in Sam's elbows, which were still resting on his palms.

65

Charlie brought his hands down, and Sam threw the ball. It sailed over the backboard.

"Wow," Charlie said. "You may be the worst basketball player in the world."

"As long as I have a title."

Charlie went after the ball. When he came back, Sam was balanced on one foot, his limbs contorted into a pseudo–tai chi pose. "Freak," Charlie said. "Want to try again?"

"Yeah." Sam took the ball from him and began dribbling awkwardly. "In fact, let's not leave this court until I make a basket."

Charlie groaned. "Oh my god, we're gonna starve to death out here. They're gonna find our skeletons in a heap on the ground."

"No, they won't," Sam said. "Watch this." He held the ball with one hand and waved his other hand at it, as if casting a spell.

"I repeat," Charlie said, "freak," as Sam turned himself toward the basket, closed his eyes, and performed a very sloppy and ridiculous-looking granny shot.

The ball arced high up into the air, dropped, and passed through the hoop without a sound.

"Holy crap!" Charlie said. He burst out laughing. "*Look!* You made the shot!"

Sam opened his eyes. "I did?"

"Yes! I can't believe you did that!"

"I made the shot!" Sam said. He grabbed hold of Charlie by the shoulders and crunched their chests together, then broke into a victory dance. "I made the shot! I made the shot!"

"I'm gonna start calling you Granny."

"You're gonna start calling me Mr. Made the Shot!" Sam said, grinning. "Let's play horse—unless you're afraid you'll lose."

"Ha! *My* name, in case you didn't know, is Mr. Kick Your Butt." They were constantly coming up with names for themselves that summer, and calling each other crazy variations on whatever they'd come up with.

A year later, they weren't calling each other anything at all.

Sam just told him one day—over the phone, with a strange quiver in his voice—that he didn't want to hang out anymore. Charlie was shocked. Then, almost immediately, he became mad. "Why not?"

"Just because," Sam said.

"Well . . . that's not a reason!"

"It's reason enough. I just don't want to hang out anymore, okay?"

"Well, then, screw you!" he hollered, and slammed down the phone. A minute later he tried to call back, but Sam didn't answer.

That next week, at school, he saw Sam across the commons. They made eye contact, but Charlie turned away, and when he looked back, Sam was walking off toward the cafeteria. After that, it became easier not to say hi. It became a predecided thing, something that hurt and that constantly bugged him, but something that just . . . stuck.

Standing at the free-throw line now, he took another shot and made it. He took another one, and made it. He took a third, and made it. Three for three.

He'd known a kid named Layton Bingham once. Layton's family had moved in next door to Charlie, and because he and Layton were both ten years old and were living just feet apart, they started playing together. It took Charlie quite a while to realize that Layton was almost always getting angry, throwing fits, making fun of him, or waving some new toy in Charlie's face and then refusing to let him touch it. It struck Charlie one day like a splash of cool water in his face: He didn't like Layton Bingham. He'd never liked Layton Bingham. He wasn't going to be Layton's friend any longer. He let Layton know, face-to-face, and that had been the end of it.

Had the same thing happened with Sam? Maybe Sam had just realized one day that he didn't like Charlie, that he'd *never* really liked him, and that was it. End of story. Maybe Charlie hadn't been as good a friend as he thought. Or maybe he'd teased Sam too much. It had always seemed like it was in good fun, and Sam had done his share of teasing back, but never as much as Charlie, who could really lay it on thick when he got going. Maybe it had always bugged the hell out of Sam and he'd just never said anything about it.

Whatever. Not whatever; he missed Sam. It would have been nice to have been able to talk to Sam when his mother got sick, and especially after she died. But what was he going to do about it now? There wasn't anything he *could* do. Besides, he had more important things to think about than a friend who had bailed on him over a year ago. Sometimes it was all he could do to keep his mind from ricocheting like a pinball, what with worrying about his father, about his debt to Derrick Harding, about his lousy game, about the fact that he was getting low on pot and couldn't exactly go to Derrick for more. (*Shit, has that joined the list of worries, too? Getting more pot? Sad, Perrin. Really sad.*)

He ran toward the basket, veered to one side, and tried for a jump hook.

The ball missed the hoop entirely.

Kate sat in the passenger seat of the Volkswagen, her shoulders moving to the song on the radio. Her dark hair was pulled back in a ponytail, and she was wearing cutoff shorts and a partially unbuttoned shirt over her swimsuit. Charlie could just glimpse the bikini top inside her shirt.

"Hey, take a picture," she told him. "It'll last longer."

He grinned and turned his eyes back to the road. "You look really great."

"Thanks."

"You look like a . . . I don't know . . . like a model." *Real original. She must think I'm an idiot.*

"I wish," she said. "Models probably make a lot more than psychologists."

"You want to be a shrink? I thought you wanted to be a veterinarian."

"One or the other. There's plenty of time to decide."

"Good thing, too," he said. "If I don't get picked up by a scout this year, I'm going to need a backup plan."

"You could always coach."

Yep, she thinks I'm an idiot. "I'm not really good at yelling. Coach Bobbit yells himself hoarse by the end of every practice. Plus he just seems mad all the time. And did you notice how fat he's getting? We call him the coach potato."

"Looks-ism," she said, reminding him of that concept he still didn't understand. "You wouldn't have to be like Bobbit. Besides, he's mainly a football coach. Basketball coaches are different. They're kind of . . . academic and sexy."

"Gross," he said. "You sound a little a looks-ismy yourself. Nah, I don't want to coach. I want to play ball for a good school, then for a great team. I want to retire at thirty, and then . . ." He didn't feel like telling her about wanting to own his own island. It seemed silly, at the moment. Because he had to say something, he said, "I don't know, become an astronaut."

Kate burst out laughing. "You can't just decide to become an astronaut one day! Those people train for *years*. Most of them start off as pilots."

"I meant as a millionaire," Charlie said, embarrassed. "That's how they're going to fund the space program in the future, you know. Millionaires buying seats on the shuttle. Be nice to me and I'll get you the seat next to mine."

"Great," she said. "I can treat all the people who go crazy on Mars."

They were south of Anastasia Island now, crossing the bridge onto Summer Haven. There were plenty of beaches to choose from in St. Augustine, but Summer Haven was theirs. It was where they'd ended up on their first date four months ago, and where they'd made out for the first time. They hadn't been to any other beach all summer.

He turned off Old A1A onto a road that led to a clearing large enough to park the Volkswagen.

"Wow," she said as they got out of the car, "could this thing be any shinier? You must wash it twice a week."

"Almost," Charlie said, grinning.

"Maybe you should detail cars for a living."

"You really have high hopes for me, don't you? I don't want to clean other people's cars. Just mine." He grabbed their blanket and towels out of the backseat, and they headed down the footpath toward the beach.

They picked a spot as far away from other people as possible. Charlie unfolded the blanket while Kate took off her shirt and cutoffs. The lime green bikini seemed to glow against her tan. He stripped down to his swim trunks.

For a while, they just lay there side by side, soaking up the sun and listening to the surf. Then Charlie asked if she wanted to go into the water. "You go, Charlie Horse," she said. "I don't want to wash off all this sunblock."

"I'd be glad to help you put it back on."

"Go swim, smart-ass."

He grinned at her and charged off toward the water.

The waves were good. He ran straight into them, spiking his knees above the waterline until the ocean slammed into his chest, pushing him back. He dove beneath the surface. When he came up, another wave smashed into him, knocking him sideways. The next wave came and he dove for it, bodysurfing at least twenty feet before it let him go. His father had taught him how to do that. It was hard to imagine now, since the man almost never left the house, but the three of them—Charlie and his mother and father—used to come to the beach every Sunday. Charlie remembered holding his father's hand and walking out farther than he'd ever been, learning how to dive at just the right moment so that the wave caught him and shoved him toward the shore. They bought a raft at Eckerd one Sunday—it was bright yellow and had a blue rope—and Charlie had blown it up on the beach and then ridden waves that dropped him right onto the sand at his parents' feet.

His mother went out on the raft with him once. They sat together, laughing, as the waves bounced them up and down. Charlie's father had brought their camera, and he snapped two pictures in a row: photos they laughed about later and stuck up on the refrigerator, like two consecutive frames of a comic strip. In one, Charlie and his mother were perched on the raft, holding hands, looking down at the water, and trying to stay balanced. In the other, the raft was tossed upward, and only their bare legs and feet were showing, pointing at the sky as they were tipped into the water.

He jumped at another wave that brought him halfway back to shore. Then another that moved him so close, his toes dragged the sandy bottom.

Kate was propped up on one elbow, reading a large paperback. He pushed his wet hair out of his eyes and squinted at the cover. *The Story of Philosophy.*

"That's the book we had in Mr. Metcalf's class," he said.

"Yep." She glanced up at him and smiled, then looked down at the page.

Charlie picked up his towel and dragged it over his head. "I used to call it *The Story of Nytol*."

"Mm-hmm."

"Why are you reading it again? Is it on the senior list?"

"No. I just like it. I'm rereading the part on Immanuel Kant. Did you know when he was seventy and really sick, he wrote an essay called 'On the Power of the Mind to Master the Feeling of Illness by Force of Resolution'?"

Charlie couldn't follow the title. In fact, two seconds after she said it, it seemed to evaporate from his mind. "Huh," he said, drying his legs.

"Kant was an interesting guy. He liked to breathe only through his nose when he took walks. He thought he could experience nature and not get a cold, that way."

"You can only get colds through your mouth?"

"That's what he thought."

"Well, what if he already *had* a cold?" Charlie asked. "His nose would be clogged up. How would he breathe?"

Kate clucked her tongue. "It's philosophy, not

biology. It's like an idea injected into the world of facts, instead of the world of facts shaping ideas."

"Sounds like he had *issues*." Charlie dropped down onto the blanket next to her. He stretched out on his back and cupped his hands behind his head. "I was thinking about my mom, out there. She went out on my raft with me one time, and this wave just totally knocked us over. My dad took some pretty funny pictures of it."

"How's your dad doing, anyway?" Kate asked, closing her book.

"What do you mean?"

"I mean"—she seemed to search for the words—"in his grief. You know, grieving is a process. He must miss your mom an awful lot."

"I miss her, too."

"I know you do. I was just thinking about him as a widower. Losing a spouse is a whole different process from losing a parent."

"You sound like a shrink already."

"Therapist," she corrected him. "I've just been reading some things. So how's he doing?"

"I don't know. We don't really talk about it."

"You have to. It's just the two of you in the house. You lost the one person you both shared."

"I don't know," Charlie said again.

"Come on, you must talk about it *sometime*."

"We don't."

"Well, you should. It's part of the process—"

"We *don't*. Okay? We don't talk about anything, as far as my mom goes."

"Don't get mad. I'm just asking as your friend."

"I'm not mad," Charlie said. But he was. To talk about it was to talk about how his dad was turning into a hermit, and how he drank every evening, and it was embarrassing to even *think* about that stuff around Kate, much less speak it out loud. If she thought he was a lamebrain who should wash cars for a living, what would she think if she knew his dad was going off the deep end? She'd reopened her book and was staring into it now. "Sorry," he said. "It just . . . bums me out to think about that stuff."

"It's okay," she said without looking up. "When you want to talk about it, I'm all ears."

"Spoken like a true shrink. I mean, therapist."

They stayed out for another hour or so. When

they were back in the car, Charlie started to turn the ignition but stopped, let go of the key, and put his hand on the back of Kate's head. He stroked her hair and said, "You're really great, you know that?"

She pecked him on the lips. He leaned into her and kissed her back. Then kissed her again, opening his mouth over hers and sliding his hand against her hip.

After a few minutes, she said, "You know, I love your car. I really do. But sometimes I wish it was a little bigger."

"We could get in the backseat." He gestured toward the space that looked even smaller than where they were sitting now.

"It's broad daylight," she said.

"We could go . . . someplace else."

"Where, one of those seedy motels on A1A?"

Actually, he was thinking about asking her if she wanted to go to the Danforth house. There wasn't a stick of furniture in it, and the floors had gotten pretty dirty since Charlie had started smashing out the windows. She probably wouldn't want to go if she knew the condition the place was in. But they definitely could have some fun there, even if they had to stand up the whole time.

Kate was giving him a funny look. "Hello," she said, waving at him. "I was kidding. You look like you were watching a porno film in your head."

"I was *not*." He felt himself flush.

"It's okay," she said, grinning, "as long as it starred us."

He kissed her again. He wanted her to put her hand in his lap, like she had for that brief, amazing moment the last time they'd made out. Instead she squinted at the dashboard clock. "Oh my god, is it really five thirty?"

"No, that thing stopped working. There's a watch in the glove compartment."

She opened the little door and pushed her fingers through the random junk he'd accumulated there.

"So maybe I *was* seeing a little film about us," he said playfully, rubbing her arm.

"What's this?"

He looked down. She was holding a small wooden pipe.

He felt his stomach fold up. "What's what?"

"*This*." She scowled. "It's a pipe." She brought it to her nose and sniffed, then shuddered. "It *stinks*. You told me you weren't doing this junk anymore."

"I'm not!" He tried to calm his voice.

"Then why do you even have this?"

"It's from back when I *was* doing it. I forgot it was even there."

She glared at him.

"I swear!" There was at least a little truth in what he was saying: He couldn't remember the last time he'd used that particular pipe, and he really had forgotten it was in the glove compartment. He had a much better pipe and rolling papers in his bedroom at home.

Kate stared down at the stinking piece of wood. "I made it really clear when we first started going out. You can do whatever you want, dope yourself up, live in a cloud. Fine. But I'm not interested in dating someone who gets high. You can do this stuff, or you can date me. That's it."

"Kate, I *know* that. Honestly, I'm not doing it anymore. That's like a—a relic from the past. Look, give it to me." She didn't move. He took the pipe from her hand and tossed it out the open window. It vanished into the palm scrub. "See? Gone."

She didn't say anything.

"All right? Do you believe me?"

"All right," she said finally.

"Thank you." He leaned over and gave her a quick kiss on the cheek. A long, awkward silence followed, while they both just sat there, staring forward at the beach. Charlie could hear his heart beating in his ears. "You want to go to a movie at the mall this weekend?"

"Sure," she said, though her tone had flattened out some and she kept her gaze forward.

"Good," Charlie said. "Just us. Whatever movie you want."

He turned the key in the ignition.

That night, his father started crying at dinner. It seemed to come out of nowhere, and a moment later he was pinching his eyes with his fingers and it was over. Charlie sat across the kitchen table, and for some reason what he felt wasn't sadness, but fear. "Are you all right, Dad?"

"I'm *fine*." He swallowed some wine and a bite of food and looked toward the television, which was on in the next room.

"Do you . . . do you want to talk about anything?"

"Me?" his father asked. "No. You mean, how was my day, that sort of thing?"

"Y-yeah," Charlie said uneasily.

"My day was fine," his father said in a flat voice.

"Did you get out of the house any?"

His father sniffed. He shot Charlie a look. "You like that question, don't you? You ask me that almost every night."

"It's just a question."

"Well, yes, I drove to the office. Did some things around here. The usual."

The usual, Charlie thought. That meant he hadn't done anything or gone anywhere.

After his father had drifted off to sleep on the couch, he went to his room, put on some music, and settled down next to his open window with his headphones on and the fan going. It wasn't so bad, what he was doing, was it? It wasn't like he was cheating on Kate. Lots of guys he knew at school had girlfriends and tried to mess around with other girls. This was just getting high and lying about it. *Sue me*, he thought, lighting his pipe.

6.

Mr. Webber started pointing to his head long before he reached the Goody-Goody booth. Sam pretended not to see him. Standing behind the counter, he kept his eyes down on the round waffle iron and the spatula in his hand.

"Sam, how many times do I have to tell you? *Hat.*"

"Huh? Oh, hi, Mr. Webber. I was just making some waffle cones. I want to be ready for the Saturday-night rush. Did I show you my trick with the miniature marshmallows to solve the leak problem?"

"Where is your *hat*?"

"It's around here somewhere. I'll find it."

"That was an awful visual I just got, Sam. I'm crossing the food court and I see eight different eateries, and eight identical mannequins behind the counters. If I were a potential customer, I could just as easily have gone over to the Cinnabon. Or the Dairy Queen. The eye should stop at Goody-Goody. That hat's an attention magnet."

It certainly is, Sam thought. Mr. Webber was a widower and a retiree from the phone company, where he'd worked as a supervisor for forty years, and once he'd retired, he hadn't known what to do with himself. So he'd bought a frozen-yogurt franchise and supervised that. He was a stickler for rules, and he was always popping up out of nowhere. He'd worked out a whole Goody-Goody philosophy, even though there was only him and a staff of four. "Draw 'em in hungry, send 'em out happy" was one of his mottos. "A little extra topping equals a little extra business" was another. For Sam, his five days a week were pretty much a cakewalk, because there were so many eateries in the food court that he never had more than a couple customers at once. He didn't like the cleanup or the yogurt-machine maintenance, but other than that it was easy money—and a good excuse to get out of the house and away from Teddy for long stretches of time.

But the hat. What a nightmare. It was a blue base-ball cap with the top of a brown waffle cone sticking out high on one side, and the bottom, pointy end sticking out low on the other, so it looked like the cone had come down out of the sky and pierced Sam's skull at a diagonal. The cone was topped with a round, white polyester blob that was supposed to be frozen yogurt and a cherry that dangled like a tassel. And, of course, the words GOODY-GOODY were stitched across the front. Franchise stuff Mr. Webber had been delighted to receive in the mail a few weeks ago, along with a new list of suggested company rules, one of which stated that if you were behind the counter, you wore the hat. It would have been better, Sam thought, if the cone had been turned upside down, like a dunce cap.

He held out as long as he could, but Mr. Webber wasn't going anywhere until he put that hat on his head, so eventually he dug it out from under the counter and put it on.

"That's better," Mr. Webber said. "Now what's this about a miniature marshmallow?"

"You put a miniature marshmallow in the bottom of the waffle cone while it's still hot," Sam said in a flat voice, his enthusiasm gone now that he was under the weight of the hat. "It seals off the bottom so it won't drip."

"That's great, Sam. You're using your head. I like that. Now, I've got some shopping to do, but I'll be back shortly, and I don't want to see you looking like all these other mannequins, you understand?"

"Absolutely," Sam said.

Mr. Webber turned to go, but then glanced back over Sam's shoulder. "Vanilla's low," he said. Then he wandered off through the food court.

Stuck in the hat, Sam thought wearily. From the walk-in cooler he got a bag of vanilla mix as large as a king-size pillow, then climbed onto a footstool, hefted the awkward blob up, and flipped it over, twisting its spout open. A wave of milky liquid glucked out in surges, and gradually the bag got lighter.

"Pretty impressive," said a voice behind him, "for someone who has a cone jabbed through his head."

He started and turned around. "Melissa, you scared the hell out of me. You know what would happen if I dropped this?"

"Extra cleanup tonight?" She pushed her straight jet-black hair back from her face.

"Let's just say you could make a disaster movie out of it. *The Goop.* How are you?"

"The usual." Melissa shrugged. "You're still coming over Monday night, right? There're going to be six of us this time."

"Yeah, I'll be there."

"Without the hat, I hope."

"*Please.* Webber's snooping around, keeping an eye on me. It was an okay job until this cone-head thing started."

"How did I not think of that? You *are* a cone head!"

"All right. A little sympathy for your friend, okay?" Sam climbed down from the footstool. "Did you get your pictures of the Pistol Museum?"

"Two rolls. *And* they let me photograph the

inside of the old jail. I sweet-talked them. Didn't have to do that at the cemetery, though—those people don't care *what* you do."

"Very funny."

"I think I'll get something." Melissa squinted through her glasses at the flavors listed on the chalkboard. "Chocolate: boring. Mango-papaya: ick. Blueberry . . . that's what I want. Swirled with vanilla. And throw a few of those nuclear sprinkles on it."

"At your service." Sam took a medium cup off the stack.

"A small!" Melissa said. "Please, I'm a whale."

"You are *not*." He glanced around quickly, checking for Mr. Webber. "I'll give you a medium but charge you for a small, how's that?"

"Thanks. But make it a *small* medium."

Sam was handing her the yogurt when he spotted Charlie Perrin across the food court.

Charlie was with Kate Bryant. They were holding hands, walking slowly toward the Pizza Hut and the Daniel Dogs, as if undecided about which one to go to. The last time Sam had laid eyes on Charlie, he'd been running past the park at the back of their neighborhood and had seen Charlie shooting baskets. Sam had spotted him first and immediately veered away before he was noticed.

Melissa followed his gaze to the spot that was holding him transfixed.

"That's Charlie Perrin, isn't it? And Kate what's-her-name."

"Bryant," Sam heard himself say.

"Right. One of those girls who doesn't know I exist because I'm not a size four. I guess we should be social and say hi." Melissa waved at them.

"No!" Sam hissed. At that moment, he saw Charlie glance over.

"Why?" Melissa asked, lowering her hand. "Because of the hat?"

Suddenly remembering the hat, Sam yanked it off his head and shoved it under the counter. "I just don't want—don't *need* to talk to him."

"God, that's right. You two aren't friends anymore, are you? When am I going to get *that* story?"

"There isn't any story," Sam said. He was still holding the cup of blueberry-vanilla swirl; he shoved it toward her. Over her shoulder, he saw Charlie's whole body make a kind of jerk, as if he were about to wave back. But Charlie didn't wave; the move was aborted. He turned with Kate toward the Daniel Dogs, and they approached the counter.

"Wow," Melissa said. "I think we were just dissed. We were, right?"

"How should I know?" Sam snapped. "They probably didn't see us."

"Not that I care. She can stick her size four where the sun doesn't shine." Melissa brought a spoonful of yogurt to her mouth.

Hell, Sam thought, *I had to be wearing that stupid hat.* He rang up the sale, stabbing his fingers against the buttons of the cash register, and took Melissa's money. She was going on about something and he was only half listening.

". . . *so* tired of these snotty cliques that act as if the rest of the world—the average, everyday world—just doesn't exist. You know what I mean? It makes me want to punch someone."

Someone cleared his throat and said, "Can I get a small cup of mango-papaya, please?"

Both Sam and Melissa looked over. A guy was leaning against the end of the counter. His hair, so blond it was nearly white, rose up in a cool, crazy sweep off his forehead. He was wearing jeans and a light-blue, long-sleeved T-shirt with the words YOUR BLISS across the chest. He smiled, and then exhaled part of a laugh and said, "Don't punch me. I'm not part of a snotty clique, I swear."

Sam recognized him. "You go to Cernak, right?"

"Yeah. I just transferred there last semester." He held his hand out to Melissa. "Justin McConnell."

Nobody shook hands nowadays. At least, no one they knew. Melissa looked down suspiciously, as if she'd been offered a joy buzzer, then brought up her own hand. "Melissa Rudge."

"The photographer," Justin said. "I know your work from the *Fountain*."

A goofy grin spread across Melissa's face. "Wow! I'm recognized!" She pumped his hand energetically.

"You're right about cliques, by the way. They're boring and exclusive," Justin said.

Sam felt nervous, for some reason. His hands weren't near anything, but he was certain he was about to knock something over. Justin extended his own hand across the counter, and repeated his name. "I'm Sam," Sam said, shaking it. He looked at Justin's wrist. He wore a thin, dark rope bracelet.

"Sam Findley," Melissa clarified. "He works on the *Fountain*, too."

"Oh, yeah, I remember that really classy article you wrote about . . . who was it—Ms. Crockett?—retiring."

"That's . . . me." Sam wondered when Justin McConnell had entered the food court and if that moment was before or after Sam had removed the waffle-cone hat from his head.

"He's going to be editor-in-chief next year," Melissa said.

Justin nodded, impressed. "Kudos."

"Yeah," Sam said. "It's a very important position. I'm actually doing undercover work right now, a crackdown piece on the whole . . . frozen yogurt scandal." *Shut up*, he told himself. *Close your mouth.*

But Justin laughed. "Good. I love scandal. I'll be part of it, with my small cup of mango-papaya."

Sam felt himself grinning. He looked from Justin

to Melissa, who motioned with her head toward the yogurt machine behind him. "Oh!" he said more loudly than he'd intended. "Duh!" He fumbled for a cup. "So . . . you moved here from the Midwest, right?"

"Yeah. Is it obvious?"

"No, it's just what I'd heard from Teisha."

"That would be Teisha Springer," Justin said. "Next year's class president."

"You seem to know everyone."

"Hard not to know Teisha after that big-budget campaign she launched. I'm still seeing those neon-colored posters whenever I close my eyes. But I knew her before that. She was the student assigned to show me around when I first got to the school."

"Didn't you move here from one of those square states?" Melissa asked.

"Sort of. Ohio. It's not square, but it might as well be." Justin dug money out of his pocket as Sam slid the cup across the counter. "What shape do you call Florida?"

"Oh, square," Melissa said, "definitely."

Sam couldn't stop staring at him. Justin looked so

relaxed, so comfortable with himself. Sam never could have gotten his own limp hair to swoop up like that. And Justin's skin was completely clear, which made Sam remember the bump on his chin that he shouldn't have messed with earlier because it was probably even redder now. When he met Justin's eyes again, Justin was looking right at him.

"You have a wicked smile," Justin said.

The compliment (was it a compliment?) caught Sam off guard. "Wicked as in Witch of the West?"

"No. Wicked as in angelic. Sort of like bad as in good."

"Or hot as in cool," Melissa added.

"Exactly," Justin said. "In fact, you have Montgomery Clift's smile."

"He does. You're right."

Who was Montgomery Clift? Embarrassed, Sam glanced down and said, "What's your shirt mean?" He pointed to the words YOUR BLISS.

Justin did a one-eighty for them. The back of his shirt read FOLLOW IT.

"Very cool," Melissa said, nodding.

"You think? The three guys I passed in the parking lot didn't seem to agree."

"What did they say?"

"Well, two of them snickered and one of them called me a fag. I assumed it was the shirt."

Melissa groaned. "People are such assholes."

Justin shrugged. "I didn't care. I felt like saying, 'How very astute,' but I didn't think they'd know what *astute* meant."

He looked down at his yogurt and stirred it with his plastic spoon. Melissa glanced at Sam and mouthed the word *Wow*.

Sam felt his hands threaten to knock things over again. He folded his arms across his chest.

"So," Melissa said, "you're an old-movie buff."

"You could say that. How did you know?"

"Not many people go around mentioning Montgomery Clift."

"They should," Justin said. "*A Place in the Sun* is one of the greatest movies of all time."

"I just watched *The 400 Blows*," Sam blurted out, wanting to contribute something.

"Truffaut," Justin said. "It's a masterpiece. Did you like it?"

"It was great."

"I love that last, long shot where you think something awful is about to happen, but nothing does. It's so powerful."

"Hey," Melissa said, "you should come over to my house Monday night. I've been having this disaster movie fest, and a group of us are going to watch *The Poseidon Adventure*."

"I love *The Poseidon Adventure*!" Justin said. Then, in a gentle voice that sounded like it belonged to someone else, he said, "What's your name, honey?"

"Nonnie," Melissa said, getting into it.

"Nonnie, your brother's dead."

Melissa clapped. "Red Buttons! Very good!"

Justin looked at Sam. "Will you be there?"

"Me? Oh, I—yeah, I'll be there."

"Cool," Justin said, grinning. "We'll all go down together."

Melissa grabbed a napkin from the counter. She wrote down her address and phone number and handed it to Justin, who scribbled on a second napkin. This he tore in half and handed a part to each of them. "That's my phone, and my e-mail."

"Thanks!" Melissa said, tucking the paper into her pocket.

Sam just stared down, amazed that he was holding it.

"You guys are great," Justin said around a spoonful of yogurt. "I should get going, though. I've got to find my mom a birthday present. Something ceramic and nauseatingly cute. So . . . see you on Monday?"

"Definitely," Melissa said. "I'll send you the info."

"Well, it was great meeting you both," Justin said.

A moment later he was walking away from the Goody-Goody, the words FOLLOW IT receding into the food court and then out into the mall.

"Well," Melissa said, turning back to Sam, "*that* was interesting."

"Yeah," Sam said. "He's nice. You two really seemed to hit it off."

She laughed and tossed her empty cup into the trash can next to Sam's hip. "Actually, *you* two were the ones who were hitting it off. But I can pretend I didn't notice, if you want me to."

Wow. Riding his bike home from the mall, Sam could still see Melissa mouthing the word to him, after Justin's blatant admission that he was gay. It hadn't even been an admission; he'd *offered* the information. Sam had never known *any*one to just come forward with something like that before. And now Justin's phone number and e-mail address were traveling home in Sam's pocket. Never mind the fact that he'd probably never get up the nerve to use either one. It was all pretty amazing.

But another remark Melissa had made had caught him completely off guard—that crack about offering to pretend she didn't notice what was going on between him and Justin. The implication was that Sam was . . . or that Sam might be . . . *Man*, he thought, *you can't even say it to yourself!* Had he ever told her anything to imply that he felt that way? He remembered one afternoon when they'd been lying on the floor in Melissa's bedroom leafing though *People* magazine, and they'd come across an article about a hot-looking movie-star couple who were getting a divorce. "Her loss," Sam had remarked without thinking. Melissa had looked shocked. "*His* loss is more like it," she'd said. They might have been defending the husband and wife, respectively, as good spouses, even good money earners. But they might also have been speaking of who was the hotter "catch." If that was the case, did it make Melissa gay, too? *You're losing it*, he thought. *The whole world is not suddenly turning gay.*

When he got home, Teddy's car was in the driveway. Sam steered his bike into the garage and went in through the kitchen.

It was after ten P.M. His mom and Teddy were sitting close together on the sofa, watching TV. They had their feet propped up on the coffee table— something Sam and Hannah weren't allowed to do.

"Hey, Nerfball!" Teddy practically shouted.

His mom shushed Teddy and said, "Hannah's asleep."

"Hey, Nerfball," Teddy said in a loud whisper. "How's the yogurt flowing?"

Kill me, Sam thought. He stepped into the living room and glanced at the television. "What are you guys watching?"

"A movie your mom's all fired up about. I think you'd call it a chick flick."

"Excuse me?" Sam's mom said. "You've been pretty caught up in it yourself."

"That's because I was figuring out the plot. They've been feeding that dead guy to the detective, I know that much. I just don't know who killed him."

"That's *not* what it's about," Sam's mom said—but in a playful tone of voice that Sam hadn't heard her use since Hannah was little.

"I'm going to bed," Sam said. "Good night." He started across the living room toward the hallway.

"Well, wait a minute. How was work?" his mom asked.

"Fine."

"Does Mr. Webber know you're about to cut down your hours because school's starting?"

"He knows."

"I still don't like the idea of you working during the school year. You don't have to, you know."

"I want to," Sam said. "It'll be fine. Good night."

"Do you want to watch some of the movie?"

"You should!" Teddy said. "Your mom's right, it's not really about a murder. It's about these two girls who want to get it on."

"Teddy!"

Sam knew nothing about the movie they were watching and told himself to keep moving before Teddy made another stupid remark. He walked across the living room and nearly made it to the hall when his anger got the best of him. He turned and said, "So it's about *mariposas*?"

"Sort of." Teddy shrugged.

"You know, you can say the word *lesbian*," Sam said. "It won't turn you into a *mariposa*."

"Good *night*, Sam," his mom said.

"Why do you let him talk that way?" Sam asked, suddenly angrier at his mom than at Teddy.

"Whoa," Teddy said. "Mr. Crankypants."

Sam glared at his mom for another moment, then stormed off down the hall.

He would have slammed his bedroom door, but he remembered that Hannah was sleeping. He dropped down onto his desk chair and glared at his computer screen. Clenching his jaw, he thought, *Stay away, just stay away.*

She did. He waited several minutes, but she never tapped on the door, never came in to talk to him. For some reason, this made him even angrier.

What could she possibly see in Teddy? How could anyone even *stand* him? Okay, so he wasn't walking around with an ax chopping people up, but he was over-the-top annoying. He practically showed up in the mornings with a napkin tucked into his collar, asking what the breakfast special was. Dropped by any afternoon when Sam's mom wasn't at work. Stuck around until late at night.

Sam thought about cranking open the window above his bed, removing the screen, and slipping outside. Maybe going for a late-night run. Hell, he could even just throw some stuff into his gym bag and take off—but where would he go? Not to his dad's, because his dad was on the other side of the Atlantic, with David. *Think big*, he told himself. *Blow the scene. You've got the money; use it. Mexico . . . Canada . . . Follow your bliss.* But he could never do that to Hannah.

Besides, the one time he'd actually tried running away had turned out to be one of the worst nights of his life.

It was over a year ago, back when his father was still living at home and his parents had been fighting heavily. If they weren't snapping at each other or having a full-blown argument, they were as silent as stones. It was awful to be around. One night during dinner, Sam asked where they were going for their family vacation that year. He was met with dead silence. He asked again.

"We're not sure," his mom told him.

"Well," he said, "it's almost summer. Shouldn't we know by now?"

"Sam!" his dad snapped. "Stop giving your mother such a hard time! It's really getting to be a problem, all right?"

His dad had been fighting with his mother for weeks; now he was suddenly sticking up for her.

Sam couldn't remember what he said back; whatever it was, it was something smart-mouthed enough to get him sent to his room in the middle of the meal. He fumed for several hours. He pounded a fist against the mattress and looked around the room for things to break, but everything was his, so what good would it do? Finally, after he was sure everyone had gone to sleep, he took the pillowcase off his bed, jammed it full of clothes and the measly contents of the Barney bank he still had from when he was little, and slipped out the window.

It was late and very dark outside. He had no idea where he was going, and as soon as he got ten feet from his house, he only wanted to see Charlie. He walked directly to Charlie's house, three blocks over.

Charlie's bedroom window was dark. Sam dropped his pillowcase behind the bushes and tapped on the glass—softly, so that Mr. and Mrs. Perrin wouldn't hear. No one came to the window. Then Sam remembered that Charlie had just gotten a new tent and had talked about putting it up in the backyard. Leaving the pillowcase beneath the bushes, Sam walked around the house and passed through the side gate.

Sure enough, there was an orange tent with dark-blue flaps pitched in the middle of the yard, its sides glowing from a flashlight within. Sam crossed the yard, and as he neared the front of the tent, which was zipped closed, he whispered Charlie's name. The light jostled against the tent walls. He whispered the name again.

Slowly the zipper came down and Charlie peeked his head through. "What are you doing here?"

I'm running away. You want to come with me? Sam couldn't bring himself to say it. The idea sounded crazy now that he was standing over Charlie. "I couldn't sleep," he said. "I thought I'd see what you were up to."

"Just . . . reading."

"You alone in there?" Sam joked.

"Yeah."

"Well, do you want to hang out?"

"Now?" Charlie looked up at the night sky, then glanced into the tent behind him. "Yeah, sure. We just have to keep the noise down 'cause my folks are asleep. Lose the shoes."

Sam stepped out of his sneakers without untying them. Then he squatted down and entered the tent.

It was warm inside. There was a sleeping bag taking up half the floor, a few magazines, and a little battery-operated camping lantern in the corner. Charlie was sitting on the sleeping bag, wearing only a pair of green Cernak High gym shorts. Sam sat down on the floor next to him. "What is this, a nudist colony?"

"It's my *tent*," Charlie said. "I'm in *nature*. What

the heck are you doing roaming the neighborhood in the middle of the night? You're gonna get picked up for being a pervert."

"I don't think so. I'm not the one camped out nude in some creepy tent."

"Doesn't this tent rock? It's almost twice as big as my old tent."

"It *is* pretty cool," Sam said. He glanced around at the orange vinyl walls and dark window netting. The tent was plenty big enough to sleep two people comfortably. The idea of running away came into his head again: He pictured the two of them on the road, living by their wits, pitching the tent at night wherever they happened to be. They could live like that for years.

Charlie stretched out flat on his back on the sleeping bag and put his arms behind his head. "You know that girl who does the Anchor Club announcements during homeroom?"

"No."

"You know her. She's got dark hair and it's kind of wavy. Her name's Kelly, or Kate, something like that."

Sam shrugged. "What about her?"

"She's *fine*, that's all. I was just thinking about her."

"I thought you were *reading*," Sam said, making finger quotes around the word.

"Shut up! She and I have the same lunch period, that's all. I was thinking about her."

"Well, I have the same lunch period with Mrs. Ornest, but I don't spend my time thinking about *that* old bag."

"Don't be a doof. You know what I mean," Charlie said.

"You're hot for her."

"If this tent had door prizes, I'd give you one."

"She's been going out with that guy on the yearbook staff, Brad Crawford," Sam said a little too quickly.

"So you *do* know who she is."

Sam shrugged again. He knew who she was—but only because Brad Crawford was so cool and good-looking, and was always hanging on to Kelly, or Kate, or whatever her name was, in the halls between classes.

"I don't think they're a real couple or anything," Charlie said.

"How would you know? You're not even sure what her first name is."

"Doesn't matter. I've seen her checking me out." Charlie gazed up at the orange ceiling. "I mean, I don't know, maybe she'd never want anything to do with a jock. Maybe to her, all jocks are stupid. A lot of girls feel that way. But I think if you really like someone, if you really can't get 'em out of your head, you owe it to yourself to at least try."

Sam felt his mouth go dry. It was a warm night, even warmer inside the tent, and he was already sweating. He could see a lacquer of sweat on Charlie's chest and stomach. "What do you mean, try?"

"I don't know. *Try.* Make your move. Maybe you say something. Maybe you just lean over one day and plant a kiss on their lips, see if there's any kind of spark. If it doesn't work out, you cut your losses and move on."

"That's pretty bold," Sam croaked.

"Well, maybe that's what it takes. If you're not

bold, you'll never know what you're missing out on."

The two of them lapsed into silence for a long moment, Charlie staring at the ceiling and Sam staring at Charlie. Then Charlie glanced over, grinning. "And I know who *you're* thinking about right now, so don't even pretend you're not."

"Who?" Sam asked, his voice rattling with nervousness.

"Oh, come on, like I even have to say it."

"Say it. Who?"

"Laura Vickers."

"Who?"

"The editor-in-chief of the *Fountain*. That totally hot redhead you spend every afternoon with after school, laying out the paper. Dude, you've got such a hard-on for her, it isn't even funny."

Sam heard himself exhale. Nothing could have been further from the truth. Yes, he spent a lot of time with Laura; she liked his work, and she was grooming him to be the next editor of the school paper. Not to mention the fact that the two of them often spent long hours picking up the slack for other, lazy staff members so that each issue of the *Fountain* could make deadline. But Sam had spent absolutely zero time thinking about Laura Vickers— or any girl, for that matter—in a sexual way. "You're whacked," he said nervously.

"Could be," Charlie said. He unclasped his hands from behind his head and folded them over his stomach. "All I'm saying is, if you want it, you've got to at least *try* to go for it. Otherwise, you'll never know."

"Maybe you're right," Sam said.

After a while, Charlie announced that he was beat and was going to sleep and that Sam was welcome to crash in the tent if he wanted to. Charlie turned the lantern out, and its light was instantly replaced with the glow of the moon, which shone through the orange ceiling of the tent enough to outline every shape like an underexposed photograph. It was too hot to sleep inside the sleeping bag; Charlie stayed on top of it and eventually rolled over onto his side, facing Sam, and began to breathe audibly in his sleep.

Sam was stretched out on the vinyl floor beside

him, wide-awake. His heart was thumping. Charlie's words were playing like a tape loop in his brain: . . . *If you really like someone, if you really can't get 'em out of your head, you owe it to yourself to at least try. . . . If you're not bold, you'll never know what you're missing out on. . . . Maybe you just lean over one day and plant a kiss on their lips.*

His mind raced through all kinds of scenarios. The craziest one had Charlie realizing, at last, that he liked Sam more than as just a friend, that he liked him as much as Sam liked Charlie, and that he wanted to find out how incredible they could be together. The most tame scenario had Sam just kissing Charlie lightly on the lips, in his sleep, so that Charlie would be none the wiser and Sam could always know how it felt, at least, to kiss his friend. His thoughts were like a roller coaster without any brakes: one hill after the other. The whole time he thought about it, he was watching Charlie, who still lay on his side, facing Sam, breathing evenly through lips that were just slightly parted and barely visible in the dim light.

. . . Maybe you just lean over . . .

He did. His face was inches from Charlie's. Then less than an inch. His entire body was trembling and his lips were so close that he could feel the warmth of Charlie's breath against them.

Then he panicked and drew back, slamming his body onto the tent's floor.

When he glanced over a moment later, Charlie's eyes were open and gazing at him sleepily. "You look totally wired, dude."

Sam muttered, "I'm fine." His chest was heaving.

Charlie grinned. "You've got Laura Vickers on the brain." He rolled over, turning his back to Sam.

You're crazy, Sam told himself. *You have to get out of this tent.* He waited until he was sure Charlie had fallen asleep again and then crept outside as quietly as possible. He stuffed his feet back into his sneakers, crossed the yard to the gate, and retrieved his pillow-case of belongings from the bushes under Charlie's window.

When he was back home in his room, under the covers of his own bed, he stared up at the swirled plaster of the ceiling and got glassy-eyed, almost tearful, realizing how close he'd come to doing something terrible. If Charlie had seen what Sam was about to do (or if Sam had actually done it!), he would have been furious. He would have pounded the shit out of Sam, or at the very least punched him and told him to get the hell out, and then he would have told who knows what to people at school. Or—what somehow felt even worse—Charlie might have *known* what had almost happened and been controlled enough not to blow up about it, in which case he might be lying in his tent right now thinking, *Sam's queer! He almost kissed me! How the hell can I face him tomorrow?*

There wouldn't be any tomorrow, Sam had decided, lying in his bed. His eyes had gone damp enough to spill over onto his cheeks, but his heartbeat had begun to level off in its thumping, and the more he'd held the thought in his head, the more he'd began to calm down. *No tomorrow. Not with Charlie. Cut your losses and move on. . . .*

7.

(We'll start with the steaks, and see where it goes.)

Charlie walked a slow circle around the Volkswagen, waving mosquitoes away from his face and glancing at his watch every few minutes. They'd picked a hell of a place to meet up. The little parking lot behind the Clam Shack was poorly lit, and there was a nasty smell coming out of the Dumpster. Nine fifteen, they'd said. On the dot. Well, it was almost nine thirty now and he was practically dizzy from having circled the car so many times.

He made a mental note to Armor All the tires this coming weekend. And it was probably time to wax again; it might just be the dim light from the pole lamp, but the fenders were looking a little dull. *Sam would ride me if he saw how much attention I give this baby*, Charlie thought. Sam had always been something of a slob. His room looked like a clothes bomb had gone off in it. And he totally didn't get the keeping-your-good-sneakers-clean thing. "Man," he'd said one afternoon, watching Charlie rub Armor All onto his basketball shoes, "if you ever get a car, you're gonna mother it to death."

"No, I won't. It'll be the happiest car in the world. I'll go through a gallon of this stuff a week."

"You're already doing that on your shoes!"

"Well, you should try it sometime. Your running shoes look like mud boots."

Had Sam seen Charlie's fantastic car? Surely he must have run past Charlie's house at least once in the past year and seen it sitting in the driveway. He might have thought it belonged to Charlie's father. Or even his mother. Did Sam even know that Charlie's mother had died?

When he'd spotted Sam the other night in the food court, Charlie's first impulse had been to wave.

His second impulse had been to go over and harass Sam about whatever that thing was he'd been wearing on his head. But that was the kind of stuff friends did, and they weren't friends. It irritated Charlie that he had to keep reminding himself of that lately.

He licked a finger and rubbed a dirt smudge off the VW's front bumper.

Headlights rounded the back of the Clam Shack. It was the twins, in their mother's Cadillac. They pulled up alongside Charlie's car. "Anthony wants to be the man next year," Troy said, as if announcing the eighth wonder of the world.

Charlie drew a complete blank in his mind. "Who's Anthony?"

"Arbizi," Taylor said, getting out from behind the wheel. "That little punk with the buzz cut. He's gone completely delusional. He wants to be point."

"Isn't that insane? I mean, it's true he's a shrimp, but he can't even keep his eye on the ball," Troy said, opening the passenger door.

Charlie couldn't think of anything he cared about less, at the moment. "So, did you get the stuff?"

"Keep your shirt on, Perrin. We got your buzz. You owe us forty big ones."

Charlie pulled the money out of his pocket. Troy took it and handed over a sandwich Baggie rolled up into a cylinder.

"Thanks, guys."

"Our pleasure," Taylor said.

"Yeah, our pleasure." Troy threw a fake punch through the open window. His fist came inches from Charlie's face. "We love being errand boys. We're thinking of charging a fee."

"A *double* fee," Taylor said.

"Well . . ." Charlie looked down at the Baggie, then tucked it into his back pocket. He didn't want to prolong this, standing around some stinky parking lot with the twins. "Thanks again." He started for his car.

"Wait, we have a message for you," Troy said.

"Yeah. Derrick says hi, and he'll be talking to you soon."

Charlie stopped in his tracks. He looked back. "You saw Derrick?"

"Hel-*lo*. Where do you think we got the buzz? We just came from his place."

When he'd asked the twins if they could sell him some pot, it hadn't occurred to him that they'd be getting it from Derrick Harding. *Idiot*, he told himself. *Where else would they get it? He's their dealer, too. They're the ones who hooked you up with Derrick in the first place.* He felt himself nodding stupidly, as if trying to say to himself and them that everything was cool. "What else did he say?"

"You want a transcript? He said a lot of stuff. We were there for over an hour. Us and him and . . . what's that jerk's name again?"

"Wayne," Troy said.

"Wade," Charlie corrected.

"That's him. Total loser. He wouldn't exhale if Derrick didn't tell him to."

"What else did Derrick say?" Charlie asked.

"Nothing. Just hi, and that he'll be talking to you."

I really wish you hadn't mentioned me, Charlie thought. He could just picture Derrick's dark, thin eyebrows arching up when the twins told him that some of the pot they were buying was for Charlie. "I've got to go."

"Wow," Taylor said, glancing at Troy. "Guess we know when we're not wanted."

"Yeah," Troy said. "Guess we're only good for one thing."

Not even that, Charlie thought. "I've just got to get home, that's all. Thanks again, guys."

"Anytime," one of them said. "Not," said the other, and then, "Be prepared for Anthony to be point. Coach Bobbit's good friends with his parents, so it's probably going to happen."

"I'll do that," Charlie said. He opened the driver's door of the VW and dropped behind the wheel. As he started the engine, one of the twins waved good-bye; the other one flipped him a bird.

He drove down San Marco Avenue for a few blocks, then pulled over in front of a strip mall that was dark and deserted at this hour. He opened the glove compartment and was fishing for his pipe when he remembered that he'd thrown it out the window to convince Kate he wasn't smoking pot anymore. She hadn't been herself around him after that argument. The evening they'd gone to the movie, she'd been quiet, and she'd seemed only half into it when they were making out in front of her house at the end of the night. *I ought to give her a call, touch base*, he thought. He looked around and spotted a pay phone in front of one of the darkened stores.

"Hello?"

"Hi, Mrs. Bryant. It's Charlie."

"Oh, Charlie! Hello. How have you been?"

"Great."

"We haven't seen much of you lately. I know you and Kate have been spending time together, but you ought to come over now and then when Mr. Bryant and I are actually home. We'd like the chance to catch up with you."

"That would be great. Is Kate there?"

"Yes, I'll get her for you. It's a little late to be calling, though, isn't it, Charlie? I hope everything is all right."

"Everything's fine," Charlie said. He pulled the receiver away from his ear for a moment and rolled his eyes. "Everything's great. I was just wondering if Kate was around."

"I'm getting her for you. How's your father doing, by the way?"

"Fantastic."

"We've been thinking about him."

It suddenly felt to Charlie as if everyone knew his business, but they were too polite to come right out and say it. As if the walls of their house were made of clear glass. "He's okay," Charlie said. "He's, you know, keeping busy."

"That's good. It's very important to stay occupied. It keeps the heart young. Well, all right then, I'll expect to see you soon. Come for dinner one night. Bring your father."

"I will," Charlie said. He could never in a million years see *that* happening.

"Kate!" Mrs. Bryant called away from the phone. "Pick up. It's Charlie."

A moment later, Kate picked up the extension. They heard the click when Mrs. Bryant hung up the phone; then Kate said, "*She's* certainly in a friendly mood."

"Yeah, she was pumping me for information."

"Did she ask about your dad?"

"Yeah," Charlie said. "Why's the Bryant household suddenly so interested in him?"

"Easy," Kate said. "My parents know . . . used to

know both your parents, remember? My mom brought it up this afternoon—not even in a nosy way, which says a lot, for her. She just wanted to know if you and your dad were doing okay."

"Sorry," Charlie said. "I guess I'm just kind of tired and edgy. So what are you up to?"

"Reading," Kate said.

"The philosophy book?"

"No. I visit that one now and then. I'm rereading *Walden*."

"Oh, yeah," Charlie said. "Is that"—he searched his brain for the name—"Kant?" He pronounced it *Can't*, which he knew was wrong as soon as he said it, but he was glad to have come up with the name at all.

"No. It's Henry David Thoreau. You know, the guy who went off into the woods and built his own cabin?"

"Oh, that guy. He was pretty cool."

"I wouldn't call him cool," Kate said. "I'd call him brilliant. He's the guy who wrote *Civil Disobedience*. Where *are* you? It sounds like you're calling from a tunnel."

"That's the traffic on San Marco. I'm at a pay phone."

"Out prowling around?"

"I was working late at the Danforth place, but I'm heading home now."

"Oh."

Charlie couldn't tell whether or not she believed him. He said, "So, listen, the reason I called . . . I was thinking you and I should go out on a fancy date. Like, a nice dinner somewhere."

There was a pause. "Really?"

"Yeah, really. To celebrate the start of our senior year. Someplace nice, where we have to dress up. Maybe the Vargo Steak House."

"That place costs a fortune!"

"So what?"

"Well . . . okay," Kate said. "I'd love to go. When?"

"How about tomorrow night?"

"You're on," she said, and then added, "You aren't planning on luring me into one of those seedy motels afterward, are you?"

He heard the playfulness in her tone. She was coming back around. "It's been on my mind," he said. "I'm just trying to find the seediest one. Want to help me look?"

"You're crazy," she laughed. "We'll start with the steaks, and see where it goes. What time?"

"Seven," he said, "sharp." She sounded like the old Kate again, even called him Charlie Horse before hanging up. He walked back to his car feeling like he'd accomplished something. What was Coach Bobbit's phrase, when they'd played a crappy game but still had a quarter to go? *Damage control.*

That night, it was the same story from his father—the same lies about how he'd driven all over town that day. Charlie found himself more irritated than worried. On impulse the next morning, after he'd made breakfast for them both, he palmed an extra egg and placed it behind one of the back tires of his father's Buick.

At the Danforth house, he smashed cracked windowpanes with a hammer, carefully broke the old glazing compound away from the frames, and painted the wood with primer. With the window frames he'd already primed, he replaced the glass and anchored new panes with tiny metal points that stuck to his fingers and vanished from sight if they were dropped. Then he laid in fresh glazing compound and smoothed it down with a putty knife dipped in linseed oil. It was meticulous work, and it was usually very good for clearing his head and getting lost from the world for a while. Today, though, he kept thinking about Kate, about the evening they were going to have together and where it might lead, and whether or not he could talk her into coming here, to the Danforth house. He also thought repeatedly about the Buick sitting in the carport. The egg behind the tire.

He didn't want to bother cooking dinner that evening because he wanted plenty of time to get ready, so he stopped on the way home and picked up a pizza.

When he got to the house and pulled into the driveway, he saw the egg, unbroken, behind the Buick's left rear tire. *Maybe he won't lie,* Charlie thought. *Maybe he'll say he hasn't done a damn thing all day.*

His father was in the bathroom off the living room. Charlie heard the toilet flush, and a moment later the bathroom door swung open and a figure lurched forward toward the recliner. His father reached for the back of the chair. If his hand hadn't caught it, he would have fallen.

"Dad!" Charlie said, dropping the pizza box onto the kitchen counter. He started into the living room. "Are you all right? You nearly fell."

"No, I didn't," his father said, sounding grumpy. His terry-cloth robe flapped open. The sash was caught under one slippered foot. He wore his pajamas underneath. "I didn't trip, I just—this carpet bunches up, right here. I've been meaning to fix it."

Charlie took his father's elbow. "Been hitting the vodka already, Dad?"

His father jerked his arm away. "Oh, knock it off, Charlie! Stop parenting me! You barely walk in the door, and you start giving me a hard time. Do I give *you* a hard time?" The edges had been sanded off his words.

"I got us a pizza," Charlie said, stepping back.

"What kind?"

"Huh?" Charlie asked, watching him. The man was practically teetering, holding on to the chair.

"What *kind*? Pepperoni? Sausage? I'm not speaking French, am I?"

"Pepperoni."

"Let's eat," his father said.

Charlie walked toward the kitchen as his father followed. A nearly empty bottle of red wine sat open on the counter next to the refrigerator. He got out plates and poured two glasses of water. They sat down at the table.

When his father bit into a slice, half of it fell down his chin. He all but growled as he swiped at his mouth with his free hand.

Charlie looked down at his plate. "So, did you go anywhere today, Dad?"

"Yes," his father said quickly. "I drove to the office. Made some calls." He chewed as he spoke.

Charlie was surprised at how angry he felt. "You're lying!" he yelled. "I know you're lying!"

It was as if he hadn't raised his voice, hadn't said anything at all. His father chewed, swallowed, stared straight ahead. Then he picked up his water glass. It slipped out of his hand and shattered on the floor.

"Whoops," his father said. He reached for the chunks of glass.

"Don't!" Charlie shouted. "What are you doing?"

His father was bending over and trying to gather the broken glass with his fingers. The hand he was using to collect the shards left a wide red smear across the floor.

"You've cut yourself!"

"I have not," his father said. "That's a scratch."

"Dad—" Charlie was bent over, trying to reach for the glass and his father's hands at the same time. "Don't! Just don't touch anything!" The cut hand was dripping blood. "Let me get a paper towel. Don't move." He jumped up from his chair and turned his back on the craziness. When he turned around again, a wad of paper towels clutched in front of him, his father was up from the table and walking across the living room, holding his hand against his robe. "Wait!" Charlie hollered. He ran after him.

His father walked down the hall to his bedroom. "Good *night*, Charlie," he said, and then sat down on the bed, still clutching his bleeding hand.

Charlie ran into the bathroom and got the Band-

Aids from under the sink. "Don't move, Dad. Just let me get this cleaned up, will you?" He knelt down in front his father and pressed the wad of paper towels to the cut and squeezed.

"*Ow,*" his father said, as if making a casual observation.

Still squeezing, Charlie looked up into his father's eyes. "I know you didn't go anywhere today."

"Charlie, please, would you just let me . . ." He glanced at the bed he was sitting on. "Sleep?"

"Tell me you didn't go anywhere. I know you didn't move your car."

"You don't know that."

Charlie peeled back the paper towels. They stuck to the bloody thumb, and when they finally gave way, he saw the puncture wound, still bleeding. "I think you're going to need stitches."

"I am not!" his father said. He actually started laughing. "*I'm* the grown-up here. *I* know if I need stitches or not. And I don't. Give me those." He indicated the box of Band-Aids Charlie was holding. Charlie handed them over. His father fumbled with the box one-handedly, and it dropped into his lap.

The egg, Charlie thought. *Tell him about the egg.* He reached forward and took the box of Band-Aids before his father could pick it up again. There was blood on the box. "Can we please go to the hospital and get your thumb looked at?"

"Charlie—*no.*"

"Fine!" Charlie snapped. "Don't blame me if you bleed to death!" But he calmed himself, pressed the paper towels against the thumb again, and used his teeth to tear open a Band-Aid. He stretched one tightly around the thumb, then opened another, and another, until the thumb was encased and the bleeding seemed to have stopped.

"See that?" his father said, looking down at the bandages. "Just a little cut. You did a good job, Charlie." He stretched himself out until he was lying flat with his head on the pillow.

Charlie rubbed his face with both hands. He got up and started out of the room, then walked back and sat on the end of the bed. With his back to his father, he said, "Here's the thing, Dad." He rubbed his face again, and clenched his hands together. "I'm—I'm worried about you. I wanted to see if you were actually leaving the house, so I—I stuck an egg under your tire. And when I got home the egg wasn't broken, so that means you didn't go anywhere. It means . . ."

He suddenly realized he didn't want to talk about the egg. He didn't even want to talk about how his father never left the house anymore. What he really wanted to talk about was his mother.

I wish Mom was here, he imagined himself saying. *I just really wish she was here, because she wouldn't let us get so crazy. I wish we could talk about Mom!*

He looked at his father, who was breathing evenly, his head sunk into the pillow, his eyes closed. He'd fallen asleep.

"Damn it!" Charlie said aloud. He glanced down at his father's thumb to make sure the blood wasn't coming through the bandages, then walked out of the room.

Sound asleep. Probably not going to move for hours. There was no reason to cower next to the window with the fan going. Charlie dug his rolling papers out of his nightstand. He rolled and lit a joint standing in the middle of his bedroom, took a long draw, and blew the smoke toward the ceiling. *He's out of control*, he thought. *I don't even know what to do with him.* He took another hit, then put the joint out, took off all his clothes, and walked across the hall to his bathroom.

In the shower, he tried to push every thought out his head and down the drain. He dried off fiercely, as if smothering flames.

Back in his room, he stood wrapped in a towel before the mirror over his dresser. His face looked puffy but his body looked thin. He would look like hell in his basketball uniform right now. Good thing he didn't have to wear it. He lit the joint again and dug through his closet, laying out a few shirts. A couple pairs of pants. A tie (he couldn't remember the last time he'd worn one). He glanced at the clock on his nightstand. Plenty of time. Even with all that craziness, he was still ahead of schedule. *Perrin*, he thought, glancing at himself, *you're going to go the distance tonight. It's going to happen. Visualize it.* He put on a CD, took one more hit off the joint to relax, then stretched out on his bed for a power nap.

When he woke up, it was nearly ten P.M. Foggy, disoriented, he sprang out of bed and scrambled for his pants. Before he had them on, he grasped how awful the situation was. This was bad. Really bad. He had to call Kate.

But he ran down the hall first and looked in at his father, who was still sound asleep. There was no sign of blood seeping through the bandage on his thumb.

Cursing and storming down the hall, Charlie went back to his room and dialed Kate's number.

Mrs. Bryant answered.

"It's Charlie. I need to—can I talk to Kate?"

"I don't think she wants to talk to you right now, Charlie. Do you?" Mrs. Bryant said faintly, away from the phone. "No, Charlie, she says she doesn't want to talk right now."

Charlie pressed his hand against his forehead. "Mrs. Bryant, please. I just need to talk to her. I need to explain something." But what was he going to explain? That his drunk father had cut himself? That Charlie had tended to him and then gotten high and fallen asleep? He had no idea what he would say; he just wanted to talk to Kate.

There was a long stretch of silence on the other end of the line, so silent that he suspected a hand was being pressed against the receiver. Then Mrs. Bryant came back on. "I'm sorry, but Kate doesn't want to come to the phone right now. She says she'll call you. It's late now, Charlie, so I'm going to hang up. Good night."

8.

(We haven't capsized yet, have we?)

"LINNN-DAA!" Melissa wailed along with Ernest Borgnine. She crouched next to the television and thrust her arm down over the back of a dining-room chair, opening her hand toward the carpet. Then she made a fist and held it up toward an imaginary Gene Hackman. "You! Preacher! You lyin', murderin' son of a bitch!"

The rest of them clapped and hooted.

"Bravo!" Justin shouted from his seat next to Sam on the couch.

Melissa made a goofy bow, then darted back down to her spot on the floor.

They'd drawn character names, according to Melissa's rules for the film festival. Whenever the group decided a moment in the movie was worthy of a dramatic reenactment, they stopped the DVD, and the person who'd drawn the name had to get up in front of the group and act it out alongside the character. Sam had drawn Belle Rosen, the Shelley Winters character. He'd already had his big moment: getting down on his knees next to the television and clutching his chest, making choking sounds as he faked a heart attack, and then collapsing onto his back. They'd given him a standing ovation.

"More!" Justin had yelled.

"No more," Sam had said, grinning as he got to his feet. "I'm dead. Now I get to go back to my trailer and . . . eat bon-bons."

The evening had been more fun than Sam ever expected, in part because Justin had shown up—and with a 2-liter bottle of ginger ale and a jar of popcorn, to boot. "*Organic* popcorn?" Melissa had said. "So it wasn't, like, doused in nuclear dust?"

"No way," Justin had said. "It's free-range, too. No cages for those corncobs. They were allowed to walk around and socialize before they were sent to the chopping block."

"How humane." She'd turned toward the living room. "Everybody, this is Justin. Justin, that's Tonya, Ben, Lisa, and Sam."

Justin had waved at everyone, but his eyes went directly to Sam, who grinned and motioned him over to an open spot beside him.

"Sorry I'm late," Justin said, his arm grazing Sam's as he sat down. "We haven't capsized yet, have we?"

"Not yet," Sam told him. "But you missed Tonya doing her Red Buttons power walk around the deck."

Melissa stuck a baseball cap in front of Justin. "Draw a name. Cliff didn't show up, so there are still two left. You're either Acres the waiter or Reverend Scott."

Justin drew the name and unfolded it like a fortune cookie. "Reverend Scott," he read.

"Good! Acres croaks about ten minutes after the ship turns over."

Now they were reaching the end of the movie. It was time for Justin/Reverend Scott's big scene. He scooped a handful of popcorn from the bowl and funneled it into his mouth. "I'm up," he told Sam, mid-chew. "Wish me luck."

On the TV screen, Gene Hackman was perched on the scaffolding, about to make his leap for the steam valve. Justin went through a few mock stretches, then stood next to the screen, watching it. When Hackman leaped out and grabbed the valve, hanging from it, Justin pitched himself forward, grabbed the empty cookie plate off the coffee table and held it over his head with his arms fully extended.

They burst out laughing and applauded.

In this position, Justin's T-shirt was riding up, exposing a quarter moon of tanned stomach. Sam's eyes kept going down to it.

"You want another life?" Hackman yelled, and Justin yelled it right along with him, staring up at the plate. "Then take me!" He knew the lines perfectly. His voice overlapped Hackman's in stereo. He turned the plate in his hands just as Hackman was turning the valve. "You can make it!" Justin/Hackman yelled to Melissa/Borgnine. "Keep going!

Rogo! Get them through!" Then he dropped straight down onto the carpet, like a marionette whose strings had been cut.

"Encore!" Sam yelled over the clapping.

Melissa's mother entered the room with a tray of brownies. She stepped up to the television and rapped her knuckles against the top of it.

"Mom, we're watching this! It's the crucial moment!"

"I know," her mother said. She bent over a little as if listening to the TV set. A moment later, Ernest Borgnine and Red Buttons and the rest were banging at the inner hull of the ship. "See?" Melissa's mother said. "They hear me." She rapped again, and the characters on the screen went wild, banging the hull with pieces of scrap metal.

"Hey, your mom just rescued us with brownies!" Justin said as she left the room.

A blowtorch penetrated the hull, the survivors were rescued, and the brownies were passed around.

"Wow," Sam said as Justin sank back down beside him on the couch, "you're a regular thespian."

"It's in the genes," Justin said. "My parents have

been doing community theater for as long as I can remember. I don't want to be an actor, though. I want to direct."

"Direct? Wow—that's pretty ambitious."

"I want to make quiet little intelligent pictures, but I'd also love to direct a disaster film at least once in my life. Big cast, huge sets, explosions. And by the way, you weren't so bad yourself, Ms. Winters."

Sam smiled, hoping he didn't have brownie smeared on his teeth. "I've been told I give good heart attack."

"She's great in *Night of the Hunter*. Ever seen it?"

"No. Was it a disaster movie?"

"Well, that depends on who you ask. The studio would say yes. But it's great. There's this amazing underwater shot of Shelley Winters dead in her convertible at the bottom of a lake. How cool is that?"

"I'll have to rent it."

"We'll watch it together," Justin said. "I could see it a hundred times." He bit into his brownie.

Sam caught Melissa's eye across the room, and she grinned, making him nervous.

After the brownies and popcorn were gone, they

were all getting ready to leave when she tapped Sam on the shoulder and whispered, "Why don't you give Justin your e-mail address?"

"Huh?" Sam asked.

"He gave you his at the mall. You should give him yours so you guys can get together—it would be like the reunion of Reverend Scott and Belle Rosen in the afterlife."

Sam glanced behind him and saw that Justin was close enough to hear their conversation, and he felt his face flush with embarrassment. "I think I'm through being Shelley Winters for a while."

"That's so not the point," Melissa said. He glanced at Justin, who gave a little shrug and smiled.

At home later that night, Sam felt ready for anything but sleep. He could have run a circle around all of St. Augustine without getting winded, so much energy seemed to be coursing through his body. He'd finally given Justin his e-mail before they'd left Melissa's, and after checking to see if Justin had written him, he wrote Melissa an e-mail thanking her for hosting everyone, and telling her he was looking forward to *Tidal Wave*, which they were scheduled to watch on the following Monday—the last week before school started up again.

He was just about to send the e-mail when a message popped up on his screen from nickoftime: Still awake?

Sam had stared at the napkin with Justin's number and e-mail enough times to recognize his screen name. He glanced around the room, as if there were people looking over his shoulder. After a moment, he leaned forward again and typed.

SKFindley: hi

nickoftime: What's the K stand for, anyway?

SKFindley: kenneth . . . my middle name . . . what's nickoftime?

nickoftime: As in "Justin the." I thought it was a little less cocky than "JustinTime." That was fun tonight. Melissa's a blast.

SKFindley: yeah . . . she loves making a big production out of movie night . . . we'll probably have to show up dripping wet when we watch Tidal Wave

nickoftime: Then I dread the night we watch The Towering Inferno.

SKFindley: LOL . . . what are you still doing up?

nickoftime: Ugh. Part of our fence blew down after that last storm. I had to walk Dusty on a leash so she wouldn't escape.

SKFindley: dusty's a dog?

nickoftime: Yeah, a retriever as big as I am—she yanked me all over the yard. Now I'm wide-awake.

SKFindley: you should walk my dog . . . he's a fat old dachshund who can hardly move

nickoftime: My ex had a dachshund. It was fat, too. Are all wiener dogs fat?

SKFindley: ex . . .

nickoftime: Sorry. Ex-boyfriend. Back in Dayton. And I ain't datin' him anymore, that's for sure. His name was Tommy. aka Mr. Creep.

SKFindley: oh . . . cool . . . well, not cool, i guess . . . but you know

nickoftime: Didn't mean to just spit that out or make you uncomfortable. I tend to just talk about—whatever. If I like who I'm talking to, that is. ☺

SKFindley: i'm totally fine with it . . . comfortable with the topic, i mean

nickoftime: Really?

SKFindley: Really.

nickoftime: t—o—t—a—l—l—y ?

SKFindley: yes! do i have to scream it?

nickoftime: No, don't. My folks are asleep.
But I thought so.

Sam sat back in his chair for a moment, one arm wrapped around his chest like a seat belt, his other hand clutching his jaw. Had he just told Justin he was gay? Was that what was happening here? He tried to think of different things he might type next, but he could really only think of one thing. He leaned forward and typed:

SKFindley: good.

The next morning, Sam felt on top of the world. He and Justin had messaged back and forth until nearly two A.M., but he still sprang out of bed at eight o'clock feeling charged up and ready to run a marathon. He felt so different that he made himself stand in front of the bathroom mirror after brushing his teeth so that he could really look at himself. On the outside, he looked the same as always. Same hair (a dirty-blond mop—would it ever get spiky?), same face (no major zits, thank god for that), same wiry body. But something was different. It must have been on the inside—it felt like an electrical surge that was somehow attached to his message exchange with Justin. When he'd crawled into bed late last night, Sam had felt like he'd spilled his guts and stamped the word GAY on his forehead; but thinking back on it now, he hadn't really admitted anything *specific*. In fact, the word *gay* hadn't been typed once by either one of them. Sam just hadn't worded anything that would give Justin the impression that he *wasn't* gay.

Giving someone the idea that you aren't interested in being thought of as not gay is practically the same as telling them you might be gay, isn't it? That was what had happened. And it felt good.

Really, though, another part of his brain said, *how can you know that about yourself? You've never had sex with anyone—other than your left hand. How can you really know for sure that you'd like it, without ever having tried it?*

Then it occurred to him that it didn't matter. He didn't have to decide what he was. Let whatever happened happen. All he had to know was that he'd had a great time seeing Justin at Melissa's and, somehow, an even better time chatting with him online, and as he left his bedroom the next morning, Sam felt as if he were walking a foot off the ground.

"Hey, Biscuit Face."

Teddy was standing at the kitchen counter, eating a bowl of cereal. His wispy hair was feathered up wildly around his head. He was wearing a long checkered jacket with a ROOF-SMART T-shirt underneath.

No—not a long checkered jacket. A bathrobe, hanging open.

And pajama pants.

"W-what are you doing here?" Sam asked uneasily.

Teddy looked down at his bowl and shrugged. "Having a bowl of cereal."

"I mean, why aren't you dressed?" He was confused. For one thing, Teddy's car hadn't been in the driveway when Sam had gotten home last night. For another, this was Tuesday, and his mom worked on Tuesdays. What the hell was this jerk doing in his pajamas in their kitchen, first thing in the morning?

"Well, the same reason you aren't dressed," Teddy said. He gestured with his spoon toward Sam's tank top and shorts. "I just got up. Most people don't jump out of bed and into their clothes. They *ease* into the day, right?"

Sam just stared at him, as if staring might make him go away. Teddy stared back and spooned cereal into his mouth.

Then his mom's voice broke the awkward silence: "Morning, Sam."

Sam spun around. She was emerging from the hall. Hannah was following, her arms wrapped around Jasbo's wiggling body. "Why aren't you at work?" he asked. "It's a Tuesday."

"Well, I know it's a Tuesday. I called in. I'm taking the day off."

"Well . . . what's *he* doing here?"

"Not feeling too welcome at the moment," Teddy said. "I can tell you that."

Sam watched his mom's face level into a more serious, annoyed expression. "I don't like your tone of voice, young man."

"Sorry," Sam said without even trying to sound like he meant it. "I just don't get it. I mean . . . did he sleep on the couch?"

His mom's face leveled out even more. She glanced at Hannah, who was bent down next to her, spilling the dog onto the carpet. When she looked back at Sam, she said, "Would you like to go back to your room and come out again, in a better mood?"

"I was in a *great* mood!" Sam snapped. He bounced his eyes from his mom to Hannah to the dog to Teddy. It was like looking at a mutated family portrait. Everything that occurred to him to say at that moment would only have made the situation worse—much worse. He stomped around them down the hall to his room and slammed the door.

This time, his mom didn't stay away. She didn't even knock. The door flew open and she closed it behind her and stepped toward his desk, where he'd sunk down into the chair in front of his darkened computer screen.

"I have *had* it with your attitude, young man," she said firmly, folding her arms.

"Too bad." This was harsh—more harsh than he'd meant it to sound. She stepped toward him, then turned away, then turned around again and practically stabbed her body down onto the end of his bed, her arms still folded over her chest. Her lips were clenched and her jaw was sliding from side to side. She was waiting for him to speak again.

He said, "So I guess you're sleeping with him."

"Sam!" His mom released her arms, and her hands seemed to move around without knowing what to do. Then they settled into her lap. She didn't look angry; she looked almost sad at that moment, and it diffused him a little. "Yes. Teddy and I slept in the same bed last night. I'm not going to lie to you about that."

"Dad's bed."

"It's no longer your father's bed, and you know it."

"Where's his car?" Sam heard himself ask. It was a crazy question: Who cared about the big oaf's car?

"Teddy was going to come over last night, but he had a flat tire. So I drove over to his house and brought him back here. He stayed the night."

"And you slept together."

"Yes."

"But you're not married, right? I mean, you didn't elope without telling anyone, did you?" He felt his eyes welling up.

"No. Teddy and I aren't married. We're dating."

"Well, if you aren't married, you shouldn't be sleeping together." Another crazy remark. Sam didn't care if people had sex when they weren't married. He just didn't want his mom and Teddy in the same bed—especially not the bed she used to share with his dad.

She reset her jaw. She studied him. "Listen, Sam. You need to understand how the world works. You need to understand that your father and I aren't together any longer."

"I understand that."

"We're separated."

"But you're not divorced."

"No. We're not divorced. But you need to understand—"

"I understand!" Sam snapped. "And I understand why! Dad's gay!"

She shushed him fiercely.

Sam lowered his voice. "He's with David now, I know that! Okay?"

The look of anger that formed on her face was so pronounced that he wondered if he'd gotten it all wrong.

"What makes you say that?" she hissed in a loud whisper. "Has your father said anything to you?"

"No! I wish he would, but he hasn't. He's too busy moving to London."

"He's not moving there. He's visiting. But what makes you say that he's—like that?"

"Because I know about it, okay? I just know. And I *really* know, so don't try to tell me it's not true."

"Have you talked to Hannah about this?"

He shook his head. "I'm not stupid. It would totally blow her mind. But, Mom, why are you *doing* this?"

The anger returned to her face. "Why am I doing what? Dating someone?"

He'd painted himself into a corner. His dad was dating David. His dad was *living* with David. Why couldn't his mom date someone? The logic of it only made him more frustrated, and he blurted out, "I mean, why Teddy? I *hate* Teddy."

She breathed through her nose. She brushed her blond hair out of her face. "Why?"

"Because he's—" *A jerk. A loudmouth. No, just say what you really want to say.* "Because he's a homophobe."

That would really get her, he thought. There was no arguing with it, given the remarks Teddy had been making lately, and what had happened in their family. But she completely surprised him by narrowing her eyes for what felt like an eternity, and then leaning forward and asking, with a sad look on her face, "Tell me something, Sam. Are you going through some phase where you think *you* might be gay?"

No one had ever asked him that point-blank—not Melissa, not even Justin during last night's online conversation. Never in a million years would he have thought that the first person to ask him this question would be his mom. Suddenly, it all felt so much more complicated. If he said "maybe"—and he wanted to say "maybe" to *somebody* at this point—his whole gripe against Teddy would seem encapsulated in maybe-gay Sam's getting his feelings hurt when Teddy made his homophobic remarks.

His mom was waiting for an answer.

Options raced through his mind.

I don't know yet.

So what if I am?

Yes! Okay? Yes!!

"*No,*" he said firmly. She still had that sad expression, so he added, "I'm *not*. I just don't like it when he says that stuff, because it's like he's insulting Dad, that's all."

The look of relief that spread over her face made him feel sick to his stomach.

"So this isn't because you think you might be—"

"*No!*" he said again.

"All right." She smoothed her hands over her knees. "Okay. I'll talk to Teddy. I'll ask him not to say things like that. But you really need to work on this, Sam. Teddy's going to be around. And you need to be able to get along with him. *You* have to do some work here, too. Okay?"

This was awful. Beyond awful. He hadn't accomplished anything other than having a fight with his mom and patching things up by lying to her. He might as well have been one of those passengers on the *Poseidon* who had no idea that *up* was the right direction to go and just kept on telling people to move *down*, toward doom. "I'll try," he said, staring at the floor in front of her feet.

9.

(You're like money waiting to happen.)

The thumb started bleeding again. Charlie was sitting next to his father, watching a tennis match on TV, when the dark spot on the bandage caught his eye. "Your hand, Dad."

His father glanced at him. "Huh? Oh." He looked down. "This is one stubborn thumb. Can you get me the first-aid kit?"

"Yeah." Charlie walked into the kitchen, a faint sensation of panic creeping into his chest. He brought the kit back to his father and knelt down in front of him to help.

They'd gone through four bandages of folded gauze and surgical tape in the past two days. When his father cut away the old gauze, the wound—surrounded now by pale, wrinkled flesh—began to seep bright red. "We should have gone to the emergency room," Charlie told him.

"I don't think they would have stitched it; it's a puncture. Cut me some tape?"

"Maybe you should get a tetanus shot."

"That's for rusty metal. This was just a piece of glass."

"Well, why won't it stop bleeding?" Charlie dangled the strips of tape from the ends of his fingers. The feeling of panic was clutching the inside of his chest. He and his father hadn't talked about what had really happened that night. They'd talked about how the glass had exploded like a grenade. They'd talked about how his father had gone to bed early and slept for ten hours, and how he hadn't been able to eat for most of the next day, but it was if they were discussing someone who had the flu and was just fighting normal symptoms. Neither one of them had mentioned the drinking.

Charlie was still angry at his father for throwing a wrench into his evening with Kate. He was mad at himself, too, for getting high (though who wouldn't want to get a little high after watching your drunk father practically bleed to death at dinner?) and for taking that stupid nap in the middle of getting ready to go. The whole evening was like one bad joke. Here it was, two days later, and Kate still wouldn't take his phone calls (and boy, was he sick of hearing Mrs. Bryant say, "I'm sorry, Charlie, but Kate doesn't wish to . . .").

More than anything, he was worried about his father. Watching the thumb get rebandaged, he fought his sense of panic, and yet couldn't help wondering if there was something wrong with his father's blood. Maybe it wasn't clotting right. Maybe he was a bleeder, a . . . whatever the name was for that condition they'd studied in human anatomy just a few months ago that he couldn't think of now if his life—or his father's life—depended on it. *What's happened to your memory, Perrin?* He imagined himself hearing it from a doctor: The results of some awful blood test were in, his father was at the start of a long illness and probably wouldn't recover. *Forget it,* Charlie thought. *Get it out of your head.* He knew he was only thinking about something so grim because of his mother. That's what *her* tests had said: There was a problem with her blood, and it was something she wouldn't recover from. And they'd been right on the money with that one; she'd stayed sick until the day she died. *It wasn't a virus, stupid. It's not like Dad could have caught it from her.* But even thinking about it made Charlie realize that, deep down, he was panicked at the idea that he might lose his father, too.

"It's just a puncture wound, Charlie." His father held up the newly bandaged thumb for inspection. "They're always slow to heal."

Charlie closed up the first-aid kit and returned it to the kitchen. When he got back to the couch, his father had returned to watching the tennis match on TV. He looked calm, almost hypnotized. "Dad?"

"Hmm?" he said, without looking over.

"Can we . . . talk . . . about the other night?"

His father blinked at the television. "There's no need, Charlie."

"I just thought it might be a good idea, you

know, if we talked about what's been going on lately." He hesitated, realizing there was a slim chance his father knew about his pot smoking, and Charlie certainly didn't want to talk about *that*. "With you," he clarified.

"There isn't any need, Charlie. Everything's going to be fine." His father sounded confident, if drowsy. He glanced over at Charlie, finally, and added, "We're survivors, right?"

Charlie opened his mouth, but no words came out. This time, he was the one who looked away, shifting his gaze to the television. He swallowed and thought, *Are we?*

He was clipping the gardenia bushes in the front of the house when he glanced over at the Volkswagen parked in the driveway. Right in the middle of the shining red hood was an enormous splatter of bird shit. "Damn it!" he said, throwing the hedge clippers down. As he crossed the yard, he peered up at the sky and saw the faint shapes of seagulls zigzagging against the blue. He'd just washed the Volkswagen that morning. It had looked perfect.

He uncoiled the hose from the side of the house and dragged the nozzle over to the car. The hit was fairly fresh; it all but vanished when the water blasted into it.

Someone had once told him that birds were color-blind, but Charlie didn't believe it. How could you even know such a thing? If he had to bet, he'd say seagulls could tell colors apart just fine. They obviously loved bright red.

He was going over the hood with a towel when a car rolled to a stop in front of the house. He looked up. It was Derrick Harding's silver Eclipse.

He felt his face draw tight across his skull.

The passenger door opened first. Wade Henson got out, his orange mullet haircut like a flame on top of a fat candle. He grinned at Charlie and made a pistol hand, casually pretending to shoot him. Then the driver's door opened.

Derrick Harding was a tall, thin guy. He wore an untucked mariachi and a pale-blue fishing cap with the bill turned up. He should have looked ridiculous in such an outfit. But somehow he looked tough. Dangerous. His face was narrow and sharp, his expression always just slightly unamused. He'd graduated from Cernak and had turned into a business what he'd already been doing since the ninth grade. He considered himself a businessman. He called his buyers "clients." He had a reputation for making things go his way.

After his mother died, Charlie had spent a couple of months in a kind of emotional hibernation, trying to interact with as few people as possible. When he came out of that, he felt like he no longer knew most of the friends he used to hang out with. He hadn't really missed seeing any of them—not like he still missed Sam—but he felt like a stranger. Then he hooked up with Derrick.

Mr. Fishing Hat. Mr. Laid-Back. For a few stupid weeks, Charlie had looked at Derrick as his new best friend. But it was mainly because Derrick had a great CD collection and was letting Charlie borrow whatever he wanted, and because Derrick was getting him high every time he went over to his apartment and sending him home with a Baggie. "I've got to start paying you for all this pot," Charlie remembered saying to Derrick more than a few times, and

Derrick would always pat him on the back and say something like, "Don't sweat it, bro. You can pay me later. It's no big deal." And, once, "If it'll make you feel better, I'll start keeping a tab with your name on it."

"Do that," Charlie had told him. "I'm good for it."

Wade was always there: sitting in an armchair in a corner of Derrick's smoky living room, rocking his big head to the music, laughing at all of Derrick's jokes, never saying much to Charlie—until Derrick started sending him around to harass Charlie about his debt.

Derrick leaned against the side of the Eclipse while Wade planted his feet apart at the end of the driveway.

"Hi, Derrick," Charlie said with less volume than he'd intended.

Derrick let his head tilt to one side. "Perrin. You disappoint me."

"Sorry I haven't been around in a while. I've been pretty busy."

Wade chuckled.

"Yeah," Derrick said. "I miss your company. You know, Perrin, this is really awkward for me, having to come to your house like this. I mean, we're friends, right?"

Charlie felt himself nod.

"Business should just . . . *flow* between friends, so that it doesn't even feel like business. But there isn't much *flow* going on lately, is there?"

Charlie exhaled and sucked in a breath. "I know I owe you some money."

"That you do. What it's up to now, Sutton?"

Wade held up five fingers.

"Five hundred bucks," Derrick said. "And, you know, it's so embarrassing for me to have to come over here like this that I feel like I should add on gas money, just to save a little dignity. But I like you, Perrin. I always have. So let's just call it five even. No gas money. No embarrassment tax. Just five. I'm about to be the new DJ at the Mix Club, and I need some equipment. You're kind of holding me up."

Charlie's mouth was dry. One day he was going to own a private island and be on ESPN discussing his record-breaking contract. Was this really happening to him? "I'll get it to you, Derrick. I'm—I'm really sorry about not getting it to you before now."

Derrick looked up at the sky. He looked down at his shoes. "You don't have it?"

"Not right now. Not all of it, anyway."

"I don't understand. Heckle and Jeckle came by my place the other night to make a purchase, and they said *you'd* called them asking if they'd sell you some buzz. So I'm confused on two counts. One, that's a hell of a markup you're paying, if you're getting it from them after they get it from me. And two, what did you pay them with? Are you broke or not?"

"Pretty much. . . ."

"Well, here I am, looking at a really nice vintage car you didn't have six months ago. I mean, it's nothing *I'd* ever want to be seen behind the wheel of, but it must have cost you a chunk of change. And six months ago, you already owed me—how much was it?"

Wade held up three fingers. He was such a loud-mouth when he was alone; around Derrick, he became a silent clerk. A yes man.

"And now it's five, and you've bought this nice car. Unless your dad bought it for you."

"Nobody bought it for me," Charlie said.

Derrick clucked his tongue. "I just can't make sense of the math."

"I'd been saving up for it. I'd been planning to buy it for a year."

Derrick clucked his tongue again.

"Wait here," Charlie said, feeling a very different sense of panic flooding his chest from the one he'd felt earlier, with his father. "I'll see what I can get." He threw down the towel he'd been using to dry the hood and walked into the house.

There were two twenties and a ten in his wallet, on top of his dresser—the money he'd planned to use when he took Kate to the Vargo Steak House. He stuffed it into the pocket of his shorts and walked back to the front of the house, his mind racing for where he might find more.

His father was taking a nap on the couch in the living room. Charlie froze for a few moments, arguing with himself silently. Then, his heart pounding in his ears, he strode back down the hall to his father's bedroom. He was sweating. His hands were shaking. He took his father's wallet off the nightstand and opened it. There was a ten-dollar bill folded into thirds. That was all.

How the hell was he going to scrape together five hundred dollars? *Sell something*, he thought, glancing around the house. But sell what?

Back outside, he kept Wade in his peripheral vision and approached Derrick, holding out the money palmed in one hand.

Derrick counted it. "Sixty. Wow, Perrin. Our friendship really means nothing to you, doesn't it?"

"I'll get the rest to you!" Charlie said. He cursed himself for bothering to glance at Wade as he said this, as if he owed Wade anything.

"Three days," Derrick said, stuffing the money into his jeans pocket. "I think that's reasonable. After that, I can only assume you've decided to throw away our friendship."

"I don't know if—"

"You don't know what?" Derrick asked. "If you can get the rest in three days? Come on. A superstar jock with a nice car like that? You're like money waiting to happen. Use your imagination. Otherwise, wow. I'm not good at this kind of thing,

Perrin, it's not my style. But it could get messy, you know?"

"I just don't—"

"Sure you do. You know."

Charlie felt himself nodding. His feet were shifting around in ways his brain wasn't telling them to.

Wade climbed back into the Eclipse. Derrick turned toward the driver's door, then glanced up and said, "Oh, and I want my Stones CD back. You've had it for three months."

He dialed Kate's number again that evening. Her mother answered—again. *Can't these people get an answering machine?* he thought. "Hi, Mrs. Bryant. It's Charlie."

"I'm sorry, Charlie, but—" Same old line. He cut her off midsentence, thanked her, and hung up.

This is why no man is an island, he thought sourly. He should tell Mr. Metcalf that. Nobody's an island because people are always getting in the way, telling you what you did wrong, telling you what a loser you are, pissing and moaning or getting all bent out of shape for no reason.

He rolled a joint, grabbed his basketball, and headed out the door. On his way past the VW, he stuck his rolling papers and half the pot he'd bought from the twins into the glove compartment. Kate wouldn't even *talk* to him, and he was supposed to pretend he wasn't getting high for her sake? He couldn't keep whatever he wanted in his own glove compartment, in his own car? Who did she think she was, Mother Teresa?

It was past nine. The neighborhood was dark and quiet, the only sound the occasional thump of his basketball against the sidewalk as he walked to the park. Once there, he stood off to the side, out of the street-lamp's light, and smoked the joint halfway down. He started to put it out, but he couldn't think of any reason not to smoke the rest of it, so he kept pulling at the wet paper until it was just a tiny roach he tossed onto the ground. The pot went straight to his head. He felt relaxed, a little dizzy. He'd never been in the park when he was high before. The court felt expansive, the rusted hoops a mile apart. He stood just dribbling the ball for a while, enjoying the sound it made when it hit the pavement. Then he started putting a little back-spin on it. Amazing. It felt alive when it hit his hands. He put more of a spin on it and caught it again, then did it a third time and his hands missed the ball entirely, so that it rolled up his chest and popped him on the chin. His teeth knocked together. "Ow!" he said. "To hell with you!" Who was he talking to— the ball? It was a funny notion, standing on a court all by himself, talking to a basketball. Only he wasn't talking to the ball at all. He was talking to himself.

He jumped and lobbed the ball toward the hoop. It popped off the rim and bounced like a rabbit over to the cinder-block wall that bordered one side of the park.

New game, he said, walking toward the ball. *It's called To Hell with You.*

He dug the ball out from behind a palmetto bush.

He didn't feel like dealing with the hoop anymore. It looked way too small for the ball to get through, anyway. To Hell with You would be a warm-up game. A fierce drill of chest passes. He walked down to a spot where the bushes stopped and it was just open wall. He dribbled, passing the ball from his right hand to his left. Then he caught it, lifted it to his chest, and as he fired it toward the wall, he said, "To hell with you."

It shot back, and he caught it: a dead, clean stop,

and a great sound, his hands against the burnt-orange rubber skin. He launched the ball again.

"To hell with Kate." As if it were metal and his hands were magnets, the ball shot straight out from the wall and into his palms.

He launched it harder. "To hell with my dad." Caught it. Launched it. "To hell with Wade." Caught it and launched it again. "To hell with Derrick."

The ball stung his palms when it made contact. He launched it as hard as he could against the wall.

Suddenly it felt as if the entire joint caught up with him. A flood of heat rose from his stomach and funneled up his neck, filling his head. *I don't want to be here*, he thought. *I should be in bed.* The three blocks to his house seemed like a long, open field dotted on either horizon by tiny houses on a treeless landscape. *Go home*, he told himself.

Then the ball appeared out of nowhere and smacked into the side of his face. The pain, just like every other sensation, was amazing.

10.

(This might sound kind of lame.)

So, Justin's e-mail began, I'm a little rusty at this, but here goes. . . .

> Would you like to hang out on Saturday?
> I wasn't thinking about anything glamorous.
> In fact, I was thinking about being totally
> UN-glamorous and going to a few of the
> cheesy tourist traps in town, because I've
> never seen any of them.
> You either a) have hit Delete by now, or b)
> are rolling around the floor laughing. If none
> of the above, then c) let me know. I'll be

hanging from a steam valve, waiting for
your answer.

Yours,
Reverend Scott

Sam stared at the screen. He was sitting at his desk,
one of his knees moving up and down. How was he
so lucky? Justin McConnell was the coolest guy he'd
met in a long time; he was great-looking and funny
and smart. Why in the world would he want to hang
out with Sam?

Sam's knees were scissoring up and down now
beneath the desk.

He glanced behind him to make sure his bedroom
door was closed. The last thing he needed was his
mom coming in and seeing an e-mail like this on his
screen. Not that the subject line read INVITATION TO A
GAY DATE, but still he didn't want her coming in contact with *anything* even remotely connected to ... that
part of him. It *was* a part of him, right? It wasn't going
to go away. And since he'd met Justin—no, be honest,
it was long before that, ever since his falling-out with

Charlie—it had been more and more difficult for Sam to pretend, even to himself, that he was attracted to girls. They left his mind whenever he started to fantasize, and now he was beginning to wonder if they'd ever really been in there at all. But his mom couldn't know about it. Not after what had happened with his dad, and certainly not after he'd denied it so fiercely during their argument a couple of days ago.

And whose business was it, anyway?

He clicked reply, then stared at the blinking cursor for a minute. Finally he typed:

> Sounds great.
> What time?
> Do you have a bike?

He clicked send, and just before the e-mail zapped off into cyberspace, it looked like the dumbest thing anyone had ever typed.

Justin's response was rendered like a telegram:

> YES TO BIKE QUESTION, BUT ALSO HAVE
> CAR   STOP

175

CAN PICK YOU UP AT NOON   STOP
NEED ADDRESS PLEASE   STOP
VERY GLAD YOU WANT TO GO   END

Sam replied with his address, logged off, and changed into his running shorts and a loose-fitting T-shirt. His Discman still wasn't working, but he didn't care. He was so charged up, he could barely get his shoes tied.

When he came back from his run, Hannah was curled up on the floor in front of the television. He heard her sniff loudly, and when he looked at her face, he saw she'd been crying.

"Hey," he said, "what's wrong?" He sat down cross-legged next to her. His mind immediately went to Teddy. Teddy had done something to upset her, Sam was sure of it.

But Hannah said, "Dad, that's what's wrong."

"What about Dad? Is he okay?"

"I guess so."

"What do you mean, you guess so? Did he call?"

"Yeah. He said for you to call him day after

tomorrow, in the morning. It's too late now because of that time-zone thing."

"Well, what's up?"

"He's staying in that stupid city another *month*."

Sam was drenched with sweat. He dragged the sleeve of his T-shirt against his forehead, but the sleeve was already soaked. "Hannah, we already knew this. He told us he was coming back late September."

"Not anymore. I talked to him, and he said he has to stay longer. Now he won't be back till Halloween."

"What?"

"Clean your ears," she snapped; she'd gotten that line from him. "He won't be back till *Halloween*. When Mom heard me talking to him about it, she practically ripped the phone out of my hand."

"And?"

"And I was just like, hel-lo, I'm talking on the phone."

"No, I mean what happened when Mom talked to him?" Sam asked.

"They had this total fight." She wiped her nose.

Her hand squeezed a button on the remote clutched in one hand, and the channels started rolling.

Sam grabbed the remote and turned off the TV.

"Hey!" she said. "What is this, National Grab Day?"

"What did they fight about?"

"She asked him—" He shushed her a little. She lowered her voice. "She asked him if he was staying over there because he wanted to, or because David was there."

"What did he say?"

"He must have said both, because she got mad and told him 'both' was 'just terrific.' Then she started talking about you and me, and she said Dad was choosing David over us."

"She said that?"

Hannah nodded.

"Wow." He wasn't sure what to think. On one hand, he was glad his mom had said it, because his dad had been gone half the summer already and it was crazy to think that he wouldn't be back till Halloween, that he was *choosing* to stay away that long. But on the other hand, Sam felt that his mom shouldn't have made the remark at all. It didn't seem fair, because it wasn't like their dad had stopped being their dad; he was just away. This was all really about David, Sam suspected. Which meant that it was all *really* about his dad's being gay.

His brain was just getting around to wondering how Hannah was piecing all this together when she asked, "Why does Dad like David so much?"

Sam swallowed. He handed the remote back to her. "David's a nice guy. What, you don't like him now?"

"I didn't say *that*." She turned the television back on and started absently clicking through the stations. "He's nice. I like him. I just don't see why Dad needs to be in London. David's the one who had to go. And why can't Dad do book research here?"

"Maybe the research is better in London right now."

She glanced at him and all but sneered her lip. "No, it's not."

"You don't even know what book research is."

"Yes, I do."

"What is it?"

"It's when you . . . when you . . . lose a book twice . . . and you search for it again." She started laughing, even though her eyes were still damp from crying. Sam cracked up, too, which made her laugh even harder.

When they'd settled down again, he asked, "So how long did the fight last?"

"Forever. Like half an hour. I don't really get why Mom's so mad, because it's not like Dad lives here now."

"Well," Sam said, "maybe she's just . . ."

He didn't want to finish the sentence. He didn't feel like sympathizing with his mom, and he was afraid of what, deep down inside, he really believed she was mad at.

A smile spread across Melissa's face when Sam told her about his plans that weekend with Justin. "I knew it," she said happily.

Sam was pouring a strawberry-banana swirl for an exhausted-looking woman with shopping bags hanging from each hand. "What did you know?"

"That you two would hit it off," Melissa said. "It

doesn't take a rocket scientist to see what's crystal clear."

"Well, we're just going to hang out downtown," Sam said. "It's not like he's my new best friend or anything." He wanted to ask her what exactly she meant by "crystal clear," but decided against it. He glanced at the woman with the shopping bags. "Topping?"

"Nuts," the woman said.

When she'd paid him and wandered away with her yogurt, Sam said, "Let me ask you something. This might sound kind of lame."

"I doubt it," Melissa said.

"Do you think Justin's . . . obvious?"

"Obvious? Obviously what?"

"Gay," Sam said. "What I mean is, do you think most people, when they glance at him, see a . . . gay person?"

"Logically, yes. He's a gay person. They look at him, and see him."

"Come on! You know what I'm trying to say."

"I *think* you're trying to ask me if people will think *you're* gay if you're seen hanging out with

Justin." She had such a calm, knowing look on her face that it irritated him.

"Well . . . yeah." Specifically, he'd been wondering if his *mother* might think he was gay, if Justin were to meet her when he came over on Saturday. "It's normal to worry about that kind of thing."

"Really? Do you have to worry?" she asked.

Sam felt his hands start to fidget. He grabbed a rag and wiped it over the counter between them, scrubbing hard, as if the counter weren't already perfectly clean. "See?" he said without looking at her. "This is exactly what I'm talking about. I tell you I'm going to hang out with Justin, and you start making little cracks about how I might be gay."

"What?" She laughed one breathy *ha*. "*I* didn't say that. *You* just said it. Talk about touchy. You have to know by now that it doesn't make any difference to me *what* you are. I don't care if you want to do it with a mailbox. But as for this whole 'does-it-make-me-gay-if-I'm-around-Justin' thing, that's your own craziness, nobody else's. Who cares what other people think, anyway?"

Sam wouldn't have thought anything could have

made him embarrassed around Melissa, but this topic, this one damn . . . *thing* . . . in his life was causing all kinds of new problems. He was still looking down at the counter, still wiping it with the rag. In a lower voice, he said, "I didn't ask you if being around him would make me gay. I just wanted to know how you thought other people might react. And you're right. Who cares?" He didn't believe this, but he said it regardless. Then he added, in a voice that didn't even sound like it was coming from his mouth, "I'm not gay, though. Just for the record."

Melissa lifted her hands, showing him her palms. "And no one on this side of the counter asked if you were."

His face was even more flushed now, but it was because he was angry at himself, not at Melissa. Of *course* he'd lied to his mom about liking guys; that made total sense. And he hadn't come right out and admitted anything to Justin because, well, that might have given Justin the idea that Sam expected something from him—or *wanted* something. And the truth was that Sam himself didn't exactly know yet what he wanted or what he was capable of doing. Or if Justin was even interested in him, that way.

But he couldn't even tell *Melissa* about any of this?

No. Not only could he not tell her, he'd just looked her right in the face and *lied* to her. His mom had backed him into a corner. But Melissa hadn't done that at all, and Sam had lied when he could have just kept his trap shut.

She said, "We should change the subject. You're staring into oblivion."

Suddenly a gray-haired figure appeared across the food court, striding toward them, and a voice called out, "Sam, hat! *Hat!*"

"I certainly am," Sam mumbled in response to Melissa, reaching under the counter for the symbol of Goody-Goody pride.

"Hello?" His father's voice sounded as if it were being broadcast from the bottom of a swimming pool.

"Dad? It's Sam."

"Sam! Hold on a second, this connection is terrible. I'm going to switch channels." There was a beep and a click. When his dad came back on the line, he sounded better. Closer. Though there was still a slight buzzing sound in the background. "How are you?"

"Fine."

"Hannah gave you the message to call, I see. I told her not to forget."

"Yeah, she gave me your message."

"So how's the last leg of your summer going? Are you getting revved up for school yet?"

"A little."

"And how's Jasbo?"

"Fat. Why are you going to stay in London all the way to Halloween?"

"Oh—so Hannah gave you the *entire* message. I told her not to tell you that part. I thought you should hear it from me."

"When I got home the other night, she was crying."

For a moment there was only the distant buzzing sound over the line. "Sam, I know it seems like I've been gone a long time—"

"You *have* been gone a long time."

"Well, I guess in a way I have, yes. But this trip is

a great opportunity for me. I've been gathering a lot of material for my book. Part of it's about the construction of Westminster Abbey, and I've had access to some valuable resources I wouldn't have at home."

"I thought you were over there because of David's job," Sam said, a little confused and slightly irritated.

"We are. David's consulting work has extended into October, which is why we're staying. But I'm also doing some valuable research."

"Are you going to move there?"

"No! Lord, no, Sam. That hasn't even been a thought. Listen to me—I'd never move to another country while you and your sister are living in St. Augustine. I couldn't stand to be that far away from you. Honestly, this is just a long trip that's turned out to be even longer than I originally thought. The worst part about it that I miss you kids so much. My gosh, you're going to be a *senior* when I see you again. That's pretty exciting, isn't it?"

Why were his eyes getting damp? Sam rubbed each of them with a knuckle and said into the phone, "So you're not moving over there?"

"Absolutely not. It upsets me that you'd even be

worried about that. This trip . . . this trip just came at a really good time for me, Sam. You know how rough the waters were there, for a while. Between your mother and me—you and I have talked about that. I mean, what I said was true, the research opportunities are great. But it's also been good for me to change my environment. Temporarily. You know, like getting some fresh air when you've been in a dusty room. That didn't come out right, I don't mean that living there with you guys and your mom was like being in a dusty room. I just needed to clear my head. Does that make sense?"

"Yeah," Sam said, staring across the living room at the mirror set into the curio box that hung over the television. In the mirror, he looked puny, like one more curio. He dragged a hand through his blond hair, and it fell back down over his forehead, limp.

"How's your mom doing, anyway?"

"You talked to her the day before yesterday, didn't you? Hannah said you two had a big fight."

His father cleared his throat. "That Hannah. She's following in your footsteps, I guess, going to be a reporter. She sure gathers her facts like a journalist.

Yes, your mother and I had words. But I'm asking you. Is she doing okay?"

"She has a boyfriend," Sam said. He hadn't planned on mentioning Teddy. But an anger was stirring around inside him now, mixing with the sadness; he didn't feel like treading lightly. "His name's Teddy. He's a real jerk."

"Ah. I didn't know that."

"He's sleeping here."

"I see. Well, I don't have to know everything about your mother's life, Sam. I was just wondering if it seemed like she was doing okay."

"I guess," Sam said, staring at himself in the mirror.

"I respect her privacy, just like I'd respect anyone else's. So this man, this boyfriend, is he . . . *living* at the house now?"

"Practically. He has an apartment, I think, but he's over here all the time."

"Hannah didn't mention that."

"I would have thought she did. She's crazy about the guy."

"Huh. Tell me something, just out of curiosity. What does Hannah call him?"

"Teddy. That's his name."

"I see. Well, you can keep me posted on any updates in that area. Why don't you like him?"

"Because he's a—" Sam caught the word *homophobe* just before it left his mouth. Suddenly he didn't want to talk about Teddy any longer. "He's just a jerk. So you're really going to stay till the end of October, Dad?"

"*Just* till the end of October. Then I'm back, I promise. To be honest, I wasn't that happy when I first heard about the extra time. I miss you kids and I'm ready to come home. But there's this research."

"You don't have to make anything up. I know why you're there, Dad."

Another pause. "What do you mean?"

"Because you want to be with David. That's why you're in London."

"I'm researching a book, Sam."

"I know. But you also want to be there with David. I *know*, that's what I'm saying. I'm fine with it."

His dad paused. "Okay. We can talk about this some more when I get home, all right?"

"I'm fine with it, because . . ."

Sam hesitated. The line went back to its buzzing sound. He understood what his father meant by feeling closed in and then suddenly wanting to change things, get some fresh air. Sam felt like a door had just been opened in front of him—*he'd* been the one who'd opened it—and he was staring through it into a totally fresh, new space. But he wasn't ready to step into it. He might never be ready.

"Because why, Sam?"

"I just miss you, that's all."

"I miss you, too. Listen, we're all doing fine. Don't you worry. It's going to be Halloween before you know it, and you'll be sick of the sight of me within a week."

"Okay."

"We should hang up now, though, because this is costing a fortune. I love you. And you tell your sister I love her, too. . . . Sam? Are you still there?"

"Yeah," Sam heard himself say from a great distance, as if he had an ocean between himself and his own voice.

"I love you."

"I love you, too."

"We'll talk soon. Good-bye."

"'Bye."

The line went dead, and the door in front of Sam slowly swung closed.

Saturday was only two days away. He had plans to spend an afternoon with Justin McConnell, and here he was walking around in a terrible mood, bothered by practically every aspect of his life. *Cheer up, would you?* he told himself. *Who wants to go on a date with someone who does nothing but mope around?* It was at least a full minute before he realized he'd thought the word *date* and hadn't immediately gotten uncomfortable or anxious. Once he realized this, he became uncomfortable and anxious.

Over the next twenty-four hours, Sam's mind seized on the fact that he was one big walking, talking contradiction. He'd lied to Melissa, one of the best friends he'd ever had, about being gay. He'd lied to his mother. He'd *almost* admitted being gay to his father but had thought better of it. And not only that, he'd decided that all of that was the right course of action. Lying was the way to go. *Keep a lid on it,* he thought, *at least until you graduate and maybe get accepted to a college somewhere far away from here, far away from Florida, where you can settle in, screen all your new friends to figure out who you can trust, and then maybe—maybe—start thinking about letting a few people know. Slowly. One at a time.* That is, assuming the whole issue didn't just dry up and blow away, so that he could wake up one day straight. Which would be a relief. Maybe.

The contradiction part came in when he thought of how excited he was about spending the afternoon with Justin McConnell.

He was determined to enjoy himself with Justin. He needed to de-stress, and the second-best way he knew how to do that was to run. He ran—twice in one day. Then, tired of his Discman being kaput, he decided finally to spend a little of the money he'd been putting away this summer. He rode his bike to the electronics store near his neighborhood.

He was looking at a display of Discmans and, next to it, a glass case filled with expensive iPods, when he heard a familiar voice.

"There's nothing wrong with it. I still have the receipt."

Sam looked over at the register. A tall guy in jeans and a Ron Jon's T-shirt was standing with his back to Sam, talking to the cashier. It was Charlie Perrin.

"Look," the cashier said, almost laughing, "you bought this three months ago—"

"Two and a half," Charlie said. "Just over."

"Fine. But the store policy is *three weeks* for returns. We can't just take back a stereo anytime someone feels like returning one."

"There's nothing wrong with it. It works fine. I have the speakers in the car."

"Sorry, our policy is firm."

"Can I—can I talk to the manager about this?"

"I *am* the manager."

Sam didn't want Charlie to see him. He moved cautiously toward the back of the store. It was a small place, tucked into the middle of a strip mall, and there was nowhere to place himself out of sight of the register.

"What if I still have the box?" Charlie asked, raising his voice a notch. "I have it at home. I just don't have the Styrofoam packing."

"Son, how plain can I make this? We don't refund purchases made over three weeks ago. I'm sorry if you're not happy with your stereo, but you shouldn't have taken three months to figure that out."

Charlie's sneakers shifted on the gray carpet. He put his hands low on his hips and turned away in frustration. When he did, his eyes landed on Sam across the length of the store.

He froze.

Sam quickly looked away, staring at the wall of Discmans. He heard Charlie huff, and in his peripheral vision he saw Charlie turn back to the cashier.

"There's nothing you can do?"

"Try the pawn shop out on U.S. 1. They'll probably give you something for it."

Just leave, Sam told himself, *while they're still talking.* He hesitated another moment, then made a beeline for the door opposite the register. He could see before he reached it that Charlie had lifted the stereo off the counter and was turning away.

They almost collided.

"Um," Charlie said, taking a step backward. "Hey."

Sam pushed the door open halfway and held on to it, focused dumbly on the stereo in front of

Charlie's stomach. After a moment, he glanced up at his face. The skin around Charlie's right eye was ashy. The cheek beneath it was swollen and red. The sight of the black eye was startling. It made Sam feel guilty, somehow, as if he'd punched Charlie himself. He pulled his gaze back and saw that Charlie was watching him stare at the eye. One of Charlie's feet had moved forward and caught the door, holding it open so that Sam could let go of it.

What happened? Sam wanted to ask. *Did you get in a fight? Did someone deck you?* Charlie's lips were parted, but he wasn't saying anything. It took Sam another moment to remember that Charlie had spoken to him, that he was waiting for Sam to reply. "H-hey," Sam said weakly.

Charlie turned his good eye down to the stereo. He looked back up. "So . . . how've you been?"

"Great," Sam said. There was so much more to say, but nothing would come. He stared at Charlie for a few more awkward seconds, then cleared his throat and managed, "I'd better go."

"Yeah, me too. This thing's kind of heavy—"

But Sam didn't wait for Charlie to finish his

sentence. He turned away and walked quickly over to where his bicycle was chained to the rack in front of the strip mall.

He knew Charlie was walking over to his car. He knew Charlie was balancing the stereo on one knee as he fumbled for his keys. Sam wanted to help him. But more than that, he wanted to get out of there fast.

He pulled the chain off his bike, climbed on, and pedaled away without looking back.

11.

(You have to **own** some of this.)

Charlie sat behind the wheel of the Volkswagen, staring up at the second floor of the dumpy-looking apartment complex where Derrick lived. He'd been hoping Derrick wouldn't be home, but there was the silver Eclipse parked in front of the building, and the lights were on in the front window of number 14. It had been three days since Derrick had come to Charlie's house—with Wade-the-barnacle stuck to his side; three days since he'd given Charlie his vague warning: Pay up or "it could get messy." Whatever that meant. Another black eye, maybe (this one caused by something other than a basketball). A broken arm. What did they always do in the movies—break a guy's knees? Give him cement sneakers and toss him into a river? In Charlie's case, it would be Matanzas Bay. Fish would eat his skin and muscles, and only his skeleton would be left at the bottom, sticking out of a block of cement, waving with the current.

But no. Derrick wasn't *that* hard-core. Besides, if he bumped Charlie off, how would he ever get his money?

This is you, Perrin. This is your life. Shaking in your shoes in front of some crappy apartment complex, worried about being offed because of your dope debt. You're a real winner.

He got out of the car and walked up the flight of concrete steps, nervously tapping the envelope against his thigh.

The Santa Claus look-alike behind the cage at the pawn shop had refused to give him more than fifty dollars for the stereo. Charlie had taken the money and had fumed all the way home about what a bad deal it was; an hour later he'd gotten over feeling cheated and had gone into hyper-drive worrying about what he owed, and had driven back to the pawn shop with his Game Boy. That had garnered him another measly thirty dollars. Then there was the forty dollars he had left over from his most recent paycheck from the Danforths. That gave him a hundred twenty dollars to put into the envelope. That plus what he'd handed Derrick the other day in the driveway came to a grand total of a hundred eighty dollars—far short of being even half of what he owed. But it was better than giving Derrick nothing at all.

He walked across the landing toward the apartment, hoping the door wouldn't open. He heard the bass thump of a stereo. *D,* he'd written on the slip of paper folded around the money, *here's all I have right now. I'll get the rest to you as soon as I can.—C.* He bent down and worked a corner of the envelope under the door. It wouldn't fit. With his other hand, he peeled up the rubber weather strip that ran along the bottom of the door and slowly worked the envelope beneath it, hoping Derrick and whoever else might be inside wouldn't notice this slow intrusion. If the door opened now, he would have to be ready to say *something*. He pictured Derrick—or worse, Wade—opening the door, catching him hunched over like this, and snatching the envelope out of his hand. Counting it. Sneering. *What are you trying to pull here, Perrin? You afraid to knock because your payment's so light?*

He could see only the last half inch of the envelope now, and peeling back the rubber strip a little more, he tapped the envelope until it disappeared.

No reason to stick around a moment longer. He stood up and walked quickly across the landing, then back down the stairs to the parking lot. He fully expected to hear his name called as he climbed into his car. But no one called his name. The door to number fourteen never opened. He started the car, backed out of his spot next to the Eclipse, and drove away.

Work it out, he thought, shutting off the engine in front of Kate's house. *Turn on the old Perrin charm*, as if there were such a thing. He angled the rearview mirror so that he could get a good look at his face. His eye looked terrible; it wasn't as dark now, but the cheek beneath it was starting to turn yellow. And his hair looked as if he hadn't combed it since he'd gotten out of bed. Nothing to be done about the eye, but he dragged his fingers through his hair, smoothing it down, and then tried out a few expressions in the mirror. The I-screwed-up. The I'm-happy-to-see-you. The I-screwed-up-and-I'm-REALLY-happy-to-see-you. The Why-the-hell-haven't-you-come-to-the-phone-when-I-called? Scratch that last one. Better to just look sorry and glad to see her, ready to work things out.

He crossed the lawn to the front porch and knocked on the door.

Mr. Bryant answered.

"Well, Charlie, what a surprise!" He offered his wide hand, and Charlie shook it earnestly.

"Hi, Mr. Bryant. Is Kate home?"

"Sure she is," Mr. Bryant said. He winced when he noticed Charlie's eye. "Ouch, that's a real mouse you've got there. Been in a fight lately?"

"Only with myself."

"Ha ha. Come in."

Charlie stepped into the foyer and stood next to a cabinet full of owl figurines.

"Kate!" Mr. Bryant called toward the living room. "Charlie's here."

He knows we're having trouble, Charlie thought. *He's on my side.* The person who rounded the corner wasn't Kate but Mrs. Bryant. She held a section of the newspaper in one hand, a pair of scissors in the other.

"Charlie," she said evenly, "does Kate know you're here?"

"Of course she does," Mr. Bryant said. "I just hollered for her. How's the squad, Charlie? You fellows putting together a winning team this year?"

"I hope so," Charlie said, smiling. "We haven't started practice yet."

"You were the best floor general in the conference last year. How many assists did you average per game?"

"About nine."

Mrs. Bryant cleared her throat. "I meant, did Kate know that Charlie was coming over?" she said, staring suspiciously at Charlie's bruised eye. "She hasn't wanted to talk to him on the phone, so I'd be surprised if—"

"It's all right, Mom," Kate said, suddenly appearing around her mother's shoulder. "I'll see him."

Mr. Bryant looked confused. "You two haven't been on the outs, have you?"

"Dad," Kate said, "it's all right."

"Well," he said jovially, "you take it easy on our boy Charlie, here. Looks like somebody's already been beating up on him." He winked at Charlie and smiled.

Charlie felt a cautious smile crimping his own mouth and offered it to Kate.

"Why don't we go outside?" Kate said. She walked between them and out the front door.

"Well, good night, Mr. and Mrs. Bryant," Charlie said.

"Say hi to your dad for me," Mr. Bryant said. "Tell him to come by the Rotary. We haven't seen him in a while."

"I'll do that."

Mrs. Bryant's voice sailed past Charlie's face like a hot wind. "Kate, if you need us, we're right in here."

Charlie ducked out of the house and heard the door shut behind him.

Kate had walked into the middle of the front yard and was standing with her arms folded, looking up at the clear night sky.

As Charlie came up next to her, he said, "What was that all about? Your mom looked like she wanted to call the police."

"Nothing."

"Have you been talking to her about me?"

Kate looked at him, nodding her head slightly. "Yes," she said. "I have. She's been a really great help, too. She's been a great listener."

"What do you mean? Last I heard, she was driving you crazy. You two were doing nothing but fighting. What exactly did you tell her?"

"Charlie, did you really come here to talk about my mom?"

Charlie swallowed. "No."

"What, then?"

His feet shifted around on the grass. He stuck his hands in his pockets. "How've you been?"

"Great," she said, sounding anything but great. "What happened to your eye?"

"Stupid accident. It doesn't hurt."

She looked both irritated and worried. After a long pause, she said, "What are you doing here, Charlie?"

"You wouldn't talk to me on the phone. I wanted to know how you were." He watched her glance at the house, as if contemplating going back inside. "Listen, Kate, things have been really crazy, lately. Really difficult for me."

"Were you high the other night, when we were supposed to go out to dinner?" she asked in a calm voice.

Charlie lifted his shoulders. He let them drop. *Be honest*, he told himself. *Put it all—or most of it—on the table.* "Yeah, I was. Just a little, though. There was a lot going on that night. Stuff you don't know about."

She unfolded her arms, stepped back from him, and sat down on the grass. Charlie sat down next to her. He waited for her to ask what kind of stuff, but she didn't. He'd just have to come out with it. "My dad's been kind of . . . messed up lately."

"Your dad?"

"Yeah. Ever since my mom died, he hasn't been himself. He hardly ever leaves the house. And he's been . . . he's been drinking at night. Sometimes more than at night. Actually, he's been hitting it pretty hard."

She brought her knees up in front of her and held on to them, her head turned away. When she looked at him again, her eyes were damp. "And this is why you've been getting high? Because of your dad?"

"Yeah. Well, I mean, not just that. But yeah."

"You know, Charlie, you can't blame your dad for what's going on with you."

"I'm not. I'm just trying to explain why *I've* been such a mess lately."

"Because your dad drove you to it?"

"Sort of."

"So he makes you smoke? He tells you it's okay?"

"No! He doesn't know about it." This was getting out of hand. "That's not what I meant."

"Does he make you lie to me, too?"

"*No.* Kate, you've got to listen to me. The other night when we were supposed to go out, when I . . . stood you up . . . I got home from work and my dad had had way more to drink than usual. He cut his thumb and it started bleeding everywhere."

"Why didn't you call and at least tell me that?"

"I was going to. But—I couldn't. I didn't want to tell you he was drinking. I was embarrassed."

"So you got high instead. While I sat in my room waiting the whole night."

"I took a couple of hits, that's all! Then I just crashed for a few minutes and accidentally fell asleep. It's been really hard for me lately, Kate."

"Well, maybe you need some help."

"That's what I'm asking for. A little understanding. I'm really sorry I stood you up—"

"I mean help as in counseling."

"What?"

"Substance-abuse counseling, Charlie."

"That's pretty radical, isn't it? We're not talking about major drugs, here. Just a little pot."

"I think sitting down with someone professional and talking about it might be a good idea. For your dad, too, from what you're telling me."

"Whoa! I'm just trying to apologize. I'm not looking for a lecture."

"I know," Kate said. Her eyes were still damp. "I don't want to lecture you. But you can't just lay all this on your father, like he's caused all your problems. That's not fair to either one of you. And it's not fair to me. You have to take some responsibility for your actions. You have to *own* some of this."

It sure was starting to sound like a lecture. He ground his teeth and felt his head bobbing slightly. "I'll work this out," he said.

"I want you to. I want everything to be okay with you, and with your dad. But I don't think I want to do this anymore, Charlie."

He felt as if a basketball had smacked into his other eye. "Huh?"

She sniffed loudly and wiped a hand against her nose. "It isn't any fun to date someone who's stoned half the time he calls you, and who may or may not show up when you have a date."

"One time!" Charlie said, feeling the panic return to his chest. "That only happened one time!" Even as he said it, he knew it wasn't true.

"Three times this summer, actually. Maybe I'm uptight, but I'm counting. Have you ever made plans with someone, and then just sat there for *hours*, wondering what happened to them—if they forgot about you, if they got in a car wreck, if they're okay? Or wondering if maybe you're a fool for sitting there, all dressed, waiting for someone to show up? It's not just that it's boring to sit around and wait like that. It's humiliating, Charlie." She bent her head forward, staring at her bare feet for a moment. Then, brushing her hair back from her face, she said, "I think you really need friends right now. You're going through a hard time, and I want to be your friend and help you get through it. But I don't want to keep dating, Charlie. Not right now, anyway. It's too—"

"Too what?" he asked, feeling his own eyes tear up. "Too much trouble?"

To his horror, he saw her nod her head gently. "Yes," she said.

"It's because I'm not smart enough, isn't it? It's because I can't talk about books with you."

"*No*, Charlie. Don't change the focus here. You're a smart guy. You just need to work on some important things, and I really think some . . . narrowing down . . . would be good for you."

"So, what, you want to break up with me? Is that what you're saying?"

"I want to be your friend."

"I've got plenty of friends!" Actually, given the path the last year had taken, he didn't have any. "You think school's going to start and you're just going to trip over some guy who isn't any trouble at all, some guy who's perfect?"

"No. I have no idea. But let's just take a rest for a while, okay?"

He wiped angrily at a tear that had spilled over and was running down his cheek. He couldn't believe this was happening.

"You can be a really great guy, Charlie. But you've got to focus right now. The last thing you need is a girlfriend who's getting upset because you didn't call. And the last thing *I* need is a boyfriend who's high."

It upset him even more to see that her eyes were dry now. She looked so resolved, so adult. "Did—did your mom put you up to this?"

"Please, Charlie! Don't insult me."

"Well, maybe you don't know," he said desperately. "Maybe you're not the expert on what we need. I mean, you're not a shrink *yet*."

She looked at him, focused on his bruised eye, and almost smiled. Then she leaned over and kissed him lightly on the cheek. "I'll talk to you in a few days," she said softly, and stood up.

His face and neck were burning. He stared forward at the houses across the street, his entire body rocking slightly. When he turned around, she had already reached the porch and the front door was closing behind her.

Hell of a day it had turned out to be. Hell of a week. His father had nearly bled to death over a pizza, he'd had to pawn what few electronics he owned to pay a fraction of his dope debt, and his girlfriend had dumped him. *And* he'd run into Sam, and had actually been glad to see him, as awkward as it was— until Sam had blown him off. He might as well have said "screw you." And what had Charlie ever done to him?

He was tired of thinking about it. *All* of it. He just wanted to get away from everyone. *No man is an island? Ha! Eat my dust, world. And once I do get my island, you can all stay the hell away from it.*

When he came into the house, his dad was sitting at the kitchen table doing the crossword puzzle. There was no glass—or bottle—in sight. Charlie pulled the orange juice from the refrigerator and swigged from it.

"Not from the carton, son," his father said. "Use a glass."

Charlie stared at him over the top of the orange juice carton. His father was actually dressed. He was still wearing his bedroom slippers, but he had on pants and an untucked button-down shirt—the furthest he'd gotten from pajamas in weeks. He'd even combed his hair. On his thumb was a single, clean-looking Band-Aid.

Charlie was in such a bad mood that it irked him, seeing his father suddenly in better shape. He didn't want to see anybody in better shape.

"You know, I'll drink from the damn carton if I feel like it. I'm the one who went to the store and bought it."

His father stopped in the middle of a word he was writing in the crossword puzzle. He laid down the pen and sat back in his chair. "That's uncalled for,

Charlie. You need to check that tone of voice. And the language."

"Maybe it *is* called for. I don't know where you've been for the past six months . . . for the past *year* . . . but you don't get to suddenly step back in and tell me what to do. *I'm* the one who takes care of *you*."

"Now just cool it, Charlie."

"*You* cool it! I can't remember the last time you said anything as a . . . as a . . . *father* to me. You hardly *see* me because you're drunk half the time! You didn't even notice I had a black eye!"

His father looked over at him, focusing. "When did you get that?"

"Two days ago!"

"How did it happen?"

"Oh—go to hell!"

"Charlie!"

He slammed the orange juice down on the counter, launching some of it through the spout. His father was getting up from his chair. Charlie stepped around him and stomped through the living room, down the hall to his bedroom. He slammed the door behind him.

Instinctively he went straight to his stereo and his headphones. But, of course, the stereo was gone. The headphones lay uncoiled like a dead snake on the floor, in the square indentation of carpet where one of the speakers used to be. "Damn it!" he hollered, throwing himself down on his bed.

A few minutes later, he heard his father tapping a knuckle on his door. "Charlie?"

Charlie lay staring up at the ceiling, his chest rising and falling heavily, as if he'd just been running line drills. "Please leave me alone."

There was a long stretch of silence. Then his father's voice came through the door again. "I will, Charlie. I'm going to let you calm down. But we can't have that kind of behavior. It's not healthy."

What do you know about healthy behavior? Charlie thought. "Fine," he said. "I'm sorry."

"You just calm down now."

"I'm *calm.*"

Another pause. "All right, son. I'm going to bed. I'll see you in the morning."

"Good night."

Charlie didn't move from the bed. He couldn't.

He hated himself. When had he become such a grouch? When had he turned into the guy who let everybody down? He closed his eyes and tried to sleep, but he only lay there wishing he could sink down into the bedspread and vanish, or at least wake up in the morning as a different person.

The first sound of breaking glass was faint, as if someone had brushed a hand against a wind chime.

The second was louder: a shatter that opened his eyes and made him sit up on the bed, wondering if he'd fallen asleep and had dreamed it.

He scrambled to his feet and went over to the window. When he drew back the curtain, he saw the silver Eclipse idling in front of the house. Two figures were standing on either side of the Volkswagen. Both were holding baseball bats.

"No," Charlie said softly, his heart pounding. He watched one of them walk around to the back of his car and swing the bat against a taillight. The other one—Derrick, he saw, recognizing the fishing hat—was poised directly in front of the VW, raising the bat over the hood. "No!" Charlie said, letting go of the curtain.

He shoved his feet into his sneakers as he heard a dull thud, like a kettle drum being struck. His father's bedroom door was closed. Charlie ran down the hall to the front of the house. He yanked open the front door and all but spilled out onto the porch.

Derrick and Wade were climbing back into the Eclipse. He started running toward them, but he wasn't halfway there before the Eclipse started to move. And it moved fast. Seconds later, it was squealing around the corner and out of sight.

He ran over to the Volkswagen. In the blue light of the street lamps he saw that both the taillights had been smashed out. There was a long scrape—made with a key, no doubt—along the driver's side, an uneven line that went all the way from the back fender to the side mirror. One of the headlights had been pulverized so that it was just an empty silver ring. And right in the middle of the hood was an angry-looking dent, deep enough to be a birdbath.

He unlocked the driver's door and sank behind the wheel. But what was he going to do? Chase them? He had no hope of catching up with them; the VW just wasn't fast enough. And what would happen if he did? There were two of them, and they had bats. The only other thing he could think to do was drive over to Derrick's apartment complex after Derrick got home and inflict some damage on the Eclipse. But where would that lead? He'd wake up a couple of mornings from now, at most, and find his car in ruins. It was a wonder they hadn't smashed out the windshield.

He sat there fuming, his hands squeezing the steering wheel. Then he spotted the piece of paper stuck beneath one of the windshield wipers.

On one side was the note he'd folded around the money he'd left for Derrick. On the other, the words *So much for friendship, Perrin.*

12.

(In the words of Hannibal Lecter, quid pro quo.)

Sam and Justin stood in the sun-baked courtyard of the Castillo de San Marcos fort, gazing into a narrow room with a single, tiny window cut into the far wall, high up near the ceiling. The room had been used as a prison cell, the pamphlet told them. Prisoners had escaped once by starving themselves until they were thin enough to fit through the window. "It's like the Count of Monte Cristo meets the South Beach diet," Justin said, making Sam laugh.

They walked the lower level of the fort, then climbed to the upper level and looked out over St.

Augustine and the Atlantic from each of the four bastions. The entire fort, they read, was made from a rock called *coquina*. It was nothing but tiny shells and lime, and when the British fired their cannons in 1702, the walls didn't shatter but just sucked up the cannonballs "like chips in a chocolate chip cookie," Sam read aloud.

Justin hung his head over the wall, looking for cannonballs. "I love it when they illustrate history with dessert metaphors. Does it say anything in there about the cannon smoke swirling like frozen yogurt?"

"Please don't mention yogurt. It's my day off."

"That's right. You're the cone-head hat guy."

Sam grimaced. "Oh, no. You *saw* me in that stupid thing?"

"Who could miss it? But don't worry. I thought it was cute, in a twisted kind of way."

"Cute as in 'look at that cute little dork'?"

Justin shrugged, grinning. "More like cute as in 'look at that cute guy wearing the goofy hat.' But I've always had a thing for men in uniform."

It was the first really *gay* thing Justin had said all

day. They'd been having so much fun that for whole minutes at a time Sam had stopped wondering if what they were on was a date, or if Justin thought Sam was gay, or if Justin even cared. As for Sam, he'd reached a surprisingly comfortable place in his mind where he was admitting—to himself, anyway—that *he* cared. He liked Justin. And not just in a you're-cool-let's-hang-out kind of way. He liked Justin *a lot.* And, most surprisingly, he found himself not caring whether or not anyone looking at them saw them as a "couple."

When Sam had opened the front door at noon, he'd immediately started laughing, because there was Justin, come to do the cheesy tourist thing and dressed *exactly* like a cheesy tourist. He wore Bermuda shorts, a T-shirt that said FLORIDA NUT (next to a little picture of a walnut on a beach towel), a sun visor, and a pair of cheap-looking, bright-yellow sunglasses. He even had a swipe of sunblock on the bridge of his nose. "I thought I'd dress the part," he'd said. Then he'd peered at Sam over the top of the sunglasses. "If anyone asks, we're from Hackensack."

Sam had worn a plain T-shirt and jeans, along with his running shoes (he wanted Justin to know he was a runner; the journalist/jock thing seemed like it might be an impressive combo). But now his outfit felt boring. To make up for it, he ducked into a souvenir shop after they left the fort and bought a ridiculous orange hat that was shaped like a thimble. He put it on and pulled it halfway down his nose, until he was looking through two circles of clear green plastic that had been cut into the brim.

"That's so sick!" Justin said, grinning. "It's perfect!"

"Where to next?"

"Lunch. I'm starving."

They climbed back into Justin's car—a dinged-up white Mustang he called the Chalkmobile—and drove to a fish place in the heart of Old Town that had a walk-up window and cement tables outside.

"I've never eaten a soft-shell crab," Sam said, squinting at the menu board through the hat's green eyeholes. "Isn't that crazy? I've lived here all my life and I've never had one."

"Don't! I watched my dad make them once, and it was horrible."

"Why?"

"Because do you know what you have to do to prepare them? You have to cut their faces off. Then you roll them in flour. Then you throw them into a pan of scalding oil, and when they start to cook, all covered in flour, they're *still moving*," Justin said, scrunching up his face.

"Eeww."

"I couldn't eat them. I probably wouldn't eat anything but vegetables if I had to watch the slaughter."

"Melissa told me plants cry when they're pulled out of the ground, but the human ear can't hear it," Sam said.

"Shut up!"

"I swear! She's always looking for new things to be depressed about, and she found this article and read it to me over the phone."

"I really didn't need to know that. And don't you wonder how long it takes for a raw oyster to die in your stomach?"

"What are you talking about? They're dead when you eat them."

"Sorry, grasshopper. They're alive. They only die

when you chew them, or when you swallow them and your stomach acid starts churning."

"No way! That *can't* be true! They're not moving around when they get to your table."

"Because they're *oysters*," Justin said. "What are they supposed to do, walk down San Marco Avenue?" He slipped into a pantomime of an oyster, walking in place and waving his right hand, then his left, a worried expression on his face. Sam tipped his hat back on his head and started laughing.

The woman behind the counter said, "If you're gonna order, order. People are waiting."

They both turned around and saw a man and a woman staring at them, unamused. Justin pushed his yellow sunglasses up the bridge of his nose. "Oh, hi!" he said. And then, "Sorry—we're from Hackensack."

Sam burst out laughing all over again.

They ate fish sandwiches at one of the concrete tables, beneath the shade of a canvas umbrella.

"So," Sam said, feeling suddenly brave, "tell me about Tommy."

"Tommy? I mentioned him, didn't I? When we were online?"

Sam nodded.

"His name's like a burp after a bad meal."

"Oh, well, we don't have to talk about him. I was just . . . curious."

"No, it's fine. Be curious. Tommy Tattenbaum. Quite a name, huh? I used to think it was cute. And to be honest, *he* was cute. Probably still is. He gave me this." Justin pointed to the thin black rope bracelet around his wrist.

Sam felt a faint stab of jealousy; he was already sorry he'd brought up the subject.

"But he wasn't a nice guy," Justin clarified. "He *seemed* nice, for a while. We were boyfriends for about a year."

"A year. Wow."

"Yeah. It's the longest I've ever dated anyone. We scandalized the high school."

"You were . . . out?"

"Well," Justin said, and took a sip of soda, "if out means showing up hand in hand at the junior prom, then yeah, we were out. He was a year older than me; I was only a sophomore. We had matching tuxes and we slow danced right alongside the class president and her date. Tommy really took a lot of flack for that, too. And I was dumb enough to think that if he took me to the prom, he must really love me. What a stupid deduction *that* was."

Sam was astounded. He felt like he'd just been born two seconds ago. Like he didn't know anything at all about the world. He said, "Wow" again, around a bite of sandwich.

"He actually looked me right in the eye during a football game one night and told me he'd realized he liked girls, not guys. Can you believe that? I just wanted to say, okay, so explain what's been going on in your room after school every Wednesday when we're supposed to be studying algebra."

"Did you say that?"

"No. I wimped out. It immediately became one of those moments I started replaying in my head, thinking of all the things I should have said. But then I thought, you know? Follow your bliss, Tommy. See where it leads you. Ten years from now, you'll be sitting there with a wife and a baby and you'll be saying to yourself, I wonder where that guy Justin is? Anyway, if you look up *whatever* in an online dictionary and click on the link, it'll take you to a picture of me and Tommy, standing in the bleachers at that football game."

Sam wanted to move on from the topic of Tommy. "Do you have other exes?"

Justin smiled. "In the words of Hannibal Lecter, *quid pro quo*."

Sam had almost half his sandwich left. He stared at it, stalling, then wolfed it down in two bites. After he'd chewed and swallowed, he said, "I haven't really . . . dated . . . anyone. Yet."

"Really? Not even a girl?"

And there it was, tossed out onto the concrete table between them. *Make-or-break time*, Sam thought. *This is the moment when you clarify what you are—and you've brought it on yourself, so don't even pretend that you didn't want it to happen—or the moment when, once again, you lie through your teeth.* He'd been getting pretty good at that, lately.

"Not even a girl," he said, staring down at the napkin he'd wadded up in his hands.

Justin was somehow right there with him, as if he were reading Sam's thoughts. "And if you could have?"

"Could have what?"

"Dated either one, which would it have been?"

"Oh. You mean . . ."

The silence was loud. It was deafening. It contained the rustling of his napkin. The car noises. The shriek of a seagull overhead, probably hoping one of them would toss a piece of fish sandwich out from under the umbrella.

"Yeah," Justin said gently. "That's what I meant—but we don't have to go there. Quid pro nothing, okay? This is a zero-stress day." He reached out and tapped Sam's hat so that it dropped over his eyes. "Let's go to the Ripley Museum."

It was crowded. They had to park at the far end of the parking lot and then wait in line to get inside the castle. But it was worth it. Justin said, "Oh, my god!" in a voice that sounded genuinely surprised when they saw the floating water spigot, which made everyone in the immediate vicinity laugh. Then Justin and Sam started playing off each other like a comedy duo, feigning amazement when they saw Beauregard the six-legged cow, the miniature replica of Big Ben made out of matchsticks, the statue of the man who'd turned his body into a candlestick holder. By the time they teetered through the revolving tunnel, the people around them were sick of their act, but they still made each other laugh.

They went from there to the Fountain of Youth. Then they drove back downtown and walked around the City Gate and the Spanish Quarter. They rode the trolley. They toured the Oldest Wooden Schoolhouse and Potter's Wax Museum.

It was getting dark and they were both out of money by the time they reached Gatorland, but Justin wanted to at least go inside and see the gift shop. With his sunglasses still perched over his nose and his visor pulled down low over his forehead, he said to the man who sold the tickets, "We're from Hackensack. We love parrots. Do you have parrots in your show—the kind that ride little motorcycles around and wear helmets?"

"No," the man said. "We don't."

"You *don't*?" He turned to Sam. "They don't have the parrots."

"I, for one, am shocked," Sam said, looking through the green plastic disks of his hat.

"'I, for one,'" Justin repeated when they were back in the Mustang. "That was hysterical." He started the car and slid a CD into the stereo.

"What's this?" Sam asked when the music started.

"Scissor Sisters. Do you know them?"

"No."

"They're great," Justin said. "They're Elton John meets the Bee Gees meets . . . Little Richard." He reached over and took hold of Sam's hand, twisting it playfully as he sang, "*Take your ma-ma out all night!*" A full verse of the song played before he let go of Sam's hand. They drove onto A1A and headed back toward Old Town.

As they turned into Sam's neighborhood, a pair of headlights splashed across the Mustang's windshield, and the oncoming car sped around them in a blur of silver, its tires squealing against the road. "Stop sign much?" Justin asked, frowning into his rearview mirror.

He reached Sam's house and pulled into the driveway. They idled for a moment. Then Justin killed the lights and shut off the engine.

"So," he said, "that was a lot of fun."

"Yeah, it was great."

"Do you want to do this again sometime? Not the tourist thing—I think I've had my fill of the Old World for a while—but, you know, just hang out or something?"

"Definitely," Sam said.

Justin had already taken off his sunglasses. He reached up now and removed his visor. Sam pulled the thimble-shaped cap off his head and held it in his lap. "Good," Justin said. "I'm glad to hear it." He fell quiet for a few moments. He stared forward at the steering wheel. "So, this is the kind of thing that used to get me into trouble back in Dayton, but I can't help it, I'm a forward guy."

"What is it?" Sam asked.

"Well, today has sort of felt like a . . . date." He glanced quickly at Sam. "And I know you haven't really committed to going to my church or anything, but—"

"What church do you go to?"

"Never mind. It's an expression. What I mean is, I'd kind of like to kiss you right now. Like, a goodnight kiss. Would that be okay?"

Sam felt his heart thumping hard. He glanced toward the house. Teddy's car wasn't in the driveway, thankfully (though, as Sam had learned, that didn't necessarily mean Teddy wasn't there), and all the windows were dark. "Sure," he said, his voice trembling around this one syllable.

There would be more talk at this point, he thought. *You're really sure? Yeah, I'm sure. Because if you're not*—but Justin was already leaning across the gap between the bucket seats, his eyes focused on Sam's mouth. Sam hesitated, then eased his head forward.

This is the part of the movie where the audience screams, "Faggots!" he thought. But he didn't care. His lips were jumping around clumsily, but then Justin's started guiding them, until their mouths were moving easily against each other. He felt Justin's hand resting lightly on his shoulder.

A few moments later, Justin pulled back. Here came the talk Sam had expected earlier. "Is this okay with you?" Justin asked. "I want you to tell me if it isn't. We have to both want to do this."

Sam couldn't think of what to say to convey *how very much* he wanted to do this. So he reached up and

231

put a hand on the back of Justin's neck and pulled him forward. This time, when their lips opened, their tongues slid against each other. Sam felt the kiss all the way down to his feet. It was like his entire body was having a conversation with Justin's body, though they were barely even touching.

When they parted, maybe a minute later, he glanced at the house.

The curtains were drawn back on one side of the living-room window. A figure wearing a long ROOF-SMART T-shirt was standing there, staring at them. *Hannah! Shit!* How in the world was he going to explain this to her? And how was he going to keep her quiet?

But an instant later he realized it was worse. Because it wasn't Hannah standing at the window. It wasn't even Teddy (which would have been bad enough). It was his mom.

"Oh, no," he heard himself say weakly.

"Oh, no, what?" Justin asked, reaching up to brush a strand of hair from Sam's forehead.

Sam knocked his hand away. "Don't!" He wanted to duck down beneath the dashboard. He wanted to vanish from the face of the Earth. She was no longer standing at the window, or at least couldn't be seen there. Justin's other hand was resting on his chest. Sam knocked this away, too. "I've got to get out of here," he managed to say, barely noticing the confused expression that had taken over Justin's face.

"What are you talking about?" Justin asked.

Sam opened the passenger door—but what was he going to do now? Go into the house? Not likely. He looked down at his feet, at the running shoes he'd worn because he'd wanted to impress Justin. Well, Justin was certainly going to see Sam as a runner now. Without another word, and without looking back, he got out and walked quickly away from both the car and the house.

When he reached the foot of the driveway, he started to run.

He had no idea where he was going; he just knew he wanted to be gone.

13.

(You don't look so good yourself.)

Charlie heard footsteps approaching, fast. He'd driven to the park at the back of the neighborhood so that he could get a better look at the car's damage under the trio of pole lamps, and his first thought was that they were coming back to pound the car some more. When he lifted his head, it wasn't Derrick or Wade, but Sam Findley slowing down to a stop several feet away.

Charlie's eyes were damp, and he felt immediately embarrassed—and angry—about having been spotted this way. Especially by Sam. "What are you staring at?" he asked, clearing his throat.

Sam ran his eyes over the battered VW. "What happened?" he asked hesitantly.

Charlie dropped his face back into his hands, which only made his sore eye throb. Looking up again, he said, "You don't want to know."

Then he realized that Sam didn't look any better than he felt. He looked spooked, even confused about where he was. His hands were shaking.

"What's the matter with *you*?" Charlie asked.

Sam seemed to snap out of a trance. "I just have to get out of here," he said quickly. "I have to go somewhere. I can't go home. I don't think I can ever go home again. *Shit!*" He started to pivot on the asphalt. He looked like he was going to jump out of his shoes.

"Take it easy!" Charlie said, getting up. "It's not that bad, whatever it is."

"Screw you! It is too! You don't know what's going on!"

"Hey—screw you back, pal. I don't know what's going on because you ditched me as a friend, remember?"

"I can't . . . I don't want to be here!" Sam said. "I just want to get as far away from my house as possible!"

He turned and started walking away. Then he picked up into a run.

"Wait!" Charlie called. "Hey, Sam, *wait!*"

Sam stopped and turned around. "What?"

"You can't just . . . run off into the night."

"Why not?"

"Well . . . it's crazy, for one thing! I mean, what's your plan? You going to run all the way to Canada or something?"

Sam seemed confused. "Maybe," he said fiercely.

Charlie glanced at the Volkswagen. "Get in," he said.

"Why?"

"Just get in, would you? We'll drive somewhere. I don't really want to be here right now either."

The idea seemed to freeze Sam where he stood.

Charlie dug his keys out of his pocket and rattled them at him.

They were crossing the Bridge of Lions when Sam tilted his head forward and started banging the heel of his hand against his brow.

"Man," Charlie told him, "you've got to chill out."

"This is so bad," Sam said. "This is so bad."

"What's going on, anyway?"

He shook his head. "I don't want to talk about it."

"Why?" Charlie asked sarcastically. "Afraid it's going to damage our friendship?"

Sam ignored him and started banging his brow again. "This is *so* bad."

"Will you give it a rest? I don't want you knocking yourself unconscious in my car. Just take a deep breath and calm down."

Sam lowered his hand. He stared at the dashboard and sucked in a lungful of air, then exhaled slowly. He glanced out the side window at the bay. "Where are we going?"

"I don't know. I'm just driving."

"What happened to your hood, anyway?"

"That's what *I* don't want to talk about."

The bridge put them onto Anastasia Island. Charlie stuck to A1A and headed south. It was hard to believe he was sitting here with Sam. The most they'd said to each other in over a year was that awkward exchange in the electronics store a couple of days ago. That left a lot of uncovered ground. But here they sat, neither one of them saying a word.

237

He rolled his window all the way down and rested his elbow on the door. He switched on—and then immediately switched off—the radio. He glanced at Sam out of the corner of his eye.

After a full mile of silence, he said, "You've *got* to tell me what's going on. You looked like you were going to blow a gasket back there."

"Yeah, well, you don't look so good yourself," Sam said. "Did the same thing happen to your eye that happened to your hood?"

"No. The eye was an accident."

"The hood was on purpose?"

"It wasn't me. Someone else did it."

They fell quiet again. Then Sam said, "Your eye looked a lot worse a couple of days ago."

"Why were you such a dick in the electronics store?" Charlie asked.

"I wasn't! I just didn't know what to say."

"I was right in the middle of a sentence and you walked away. That's pretty dickish, if you ask me."

They sailed past a police cruiser sitting at the entrance to Butler Park. Charlie checked his speed. It was fine. Then he remembered both his tail lights had been smashed out.

"Sorry," Sam said evenly. "It was just weird, that's all."

"Don't," Charlie said, staring into his side mirror.

"Don't what? Apologize? Then don't tell me I was a dick."

"Don't, don't, don't," Charlie muttered, ignoring him.

The cruiser, already shrunk down to a tiny pair of headlights in the mirror, turned onto A1A. A second later, the reds and blues were flashing, and they heard the siren.

"Damn it!" Charlie said.

Sam turned in his seat and looked behind them. "You know you've only got one headlight."

"And no taillights. Please do *not* let this be happening."

"He's got you. Just pull over."

"I can't," Charlie said.

"Why not?"

"Because I can't!" He didn't want to explain to Sam about the Baggie of pot in the glove compartment. He didn't want to explain it to anyone. He glanced over at Sam's lap. "Hook your seatbelt."

"You're not going to—"

Sam's question was answered when Charlie pressed the gas pedal to the floor. Sam hooked his seatbelt.

The cruiser was still far behind them, but gaining.

Charlie knew the VW wasn't fast enough to outrun anything. "Hold on," he said. There were other cars on the highway, but none of them close. He hit the brakes, killed the lights, and made a sharp left. Sam grabbed the vinyl strap near his head and braced his other hand against the dash. The tires squealed over the pavement.

"You're going to kill somebody!" Sam said. "You're going to kill *us*!"

"Just hold on," Charlie groaned. He knew the street. It was residential, but there were only a few houses on it, tucked out of sight. Here and there, a wood-chip–lined path was cut into the palm scrub, just wide enough for the Volkswagen. They were right next to the beach Kate liked to come to.

With the lights still off, Charlie turned onto one of the darkened side paths and steered the car into the tiny clearing where he and Kate had parked just last week. It put them almost entirely out of sight from the residential street.

"What the hell—" Sam began.

Charlie shushed him. They heard the siren approach, then saw flickers of red and blue light flashing through the leaves. The cruiser drove straight past them, following the street that Charlie knew led back out onto A1A, and the siren receded into the distance.

"Can I speak now?" Sam asked in an exasperated voice.

Charlie nodded.

"Are you nuts? You'd have gone straight to jail if they'd caught us!"

"I know."

"Well, they don't put you in jail for having a busted taillight! Why didn't you just pull over?"

Charlie's mind was racing. "We're going to have to sit here for a while. I don't know how we're going to get home. They'll be watching for us."

Sam looked out at the wall of palmetto leaves near his window. "I don't *get* it," he said. "I was having, like, the worst night of my life, and now you've screwed it up even more!"

"We'll just have to wait till it's daylight," Charlie said, thinking aloud.

"What are you talking about?"

"That cop probably didn't get my license number. He didn't pull out right away. So we'll just wait until daylight, then drive home, and tomorrow I'll replace the bulbs. They might even have taillight shells at the junkyard."

"You're *crazy*," Sam said. "Do you know that? *Crazy*."

"Everything's fine."

"Everything's *not* fine! That was a *really* stupid thing you just did."

"All right, shut up!" Charlie snapped. His hands were still gripping the steering wheel. He looked over at Sam. "All we have to do is wait it out."

"I'm not spending the night in the middle of the woods in your crappy car!"

"We don't have to," Charlie said, remembering. He opened the glove compartment and reached inside. "I just thought of something."

14.

They locked up the car and followed the footpath down to the beach. Sam still couldn't believe how quickly his day had fallen apart. He felt shell-shocked, numb, as if his brain couldn't hold on to everything that had happened over the past twelve hours.

It was low tide. The water was so far out that the beach seemed to stretch on for miles to the horizon, rippled and glistening like the damp surface of some foreign planet. There were houses tucked into the palmettos, most of them dark. The full moon rendered the sand a deep neon blue.

How could he ever face Justin again? How could he ever face his mom? He didn't want to think about it. "Are you going to tell me what that was all about, back there?" he asked, trying to put his mind on something else.

"Can we just . . . be quiet for a minute?" Charlie asked. "At least till we get to the house?"

"What house?"

"Where I work. This is Crescent Beach. The house isn't too much farther."

Sam didn't know what Charlie's job was, but as they walked side by side along the sand, he realized Charlie was right: It *was* nice not talking about anything, pretending—for a few moments, anyway— that nothing was wrong, that they were just hanging out, the two of them. Like they used to.

We could be on another planet, he thought, listening to the distant surf. *We could be the only two people on it. We've just landed, and no one else is going to come.* Childish thoughts, but he kept them to himself and was able to enjoy them as they made their way across the beach. He turned around and walked backward for a few yards, looking at the footprints they'd made in the bluish sand.

"You're going to fall on your ass," Charlie said. And then, "Here's the house."

Sam looked to where he was pointing. The house was small and completely dark. They mounted a short boardwalk that led right up to the back porch.

"This is where you work?"

Charlie nodded. "It belongs to a family that must be loaded, because they don't even live here yet but they're having it fixed up."

"You're house-sitting?"

"I'm painting the inside. And redoing the windows." Charlie dug his key ring out of his pocket and unlocked the sliding glass door. They stepped inside.

There was no furniture. There were no curtains on the windows. The living room was completely empty except for a ladder, a canvas tarp spread across one corner of the floor, some paint cans, and a toolbox. "All this stuff is yours?" Sam asked. He had no idea Charlie could do this kind of work. It made him feel ridiculous to think that all he did for a job was serve yogurt.

Charlie walked over to the tarp and kicked at it. "Yeah. Well, the Danforths paid for all the supplies. I just do the work."

"Where are they?"

"In Pensacola. They don't seem to be in any hurry to move here, either. Like I said, they must be loaded." He smoothed the tarp out with his shoe and looked around, wiping his hands on his hips. "We can hang out here till morning."

We could hang out here forever, Sam thought.

He was already forgetting that officially they weren't friends. How long would it take for anyone to find them? If the Danforths were all the way over in Pensacola, and the car was stashed away, no one would know where they were, which was fine with Sam. And it might be fine with Charlie, too, because something was up; even before the police came after them, Charlie had been upset.

"Hey, watch this." Charlie bent down and opened the toolbox. He pulled out a hammer and walked over to a large picture window made up of dozens of panes of glass. "See this pane? See the crack down the middle of it?"

Sam moved closer and squinted. "Yeah."

"Here's the best part of my job," Charlie said. Then he lifted the hammer and smashed it against the windowpane, shattering it. The shards of glass flew out into the yard.

"What did you do that for?"

"It's my job," Charlie said, smiling. "I'm replacing all the cracked windows and reglazing them. Here, you try it."

"I don't think so."

"Take the hammer. Here's another pane with a crack in it."

"It's hardly cracked at all."

"I *have* to replace every cracked pane. It's my job. Go ahead."

Sam took the hammer from his hand, but he didn't do anything with it. Charlie took hold of his wrist and raised his hand until the hammer was poised in front of the cracked pane. "You don't really want me to do this," Sam said.

"Of course I do. I've already bought the new glass."

Sam looked at him. Charlie nodded. Sam swung the hammer, but not hard enough; it bounced off the window as if the glass were rubber.

"Come on. *Smash* it."

He swung again. This time, the glass shattered. It was a good feeling, somehow, hearing the crash and seeing the immediate result of open, jagged space within the wooden frame.

"You're a natural," Charlie said absently. He stepped back, then dropped down and sat cross-legged next to the tarp.

"You're just going to leave it broken?"

"I'll fix it tomorrow." He was no longer looking at the picture window. He was staring at the bare floor in front of him. "This is a little weird, isn't it?"

"What?"

"The two of us, in the same room. I haven't talked to you in, what, a year? More than a year?"

"That doesn't have to make it weird, does it?"

"Dude, you basically told me to go to hell."

"I did not!" Sam felt nervous, all of a sudden. He dropped the hammer back into the toolbox and walked to the other side of the empty room.

"You might as well have," Charlie said.

Sam sat down on the floor. "Let's focus on the now. Are you going to tell me what's going on, or not? You've turned me into a fugitive from the law. We're on the lam here. I think I have a right to know *why*."

Charlie almost laughed. "We're not on the lam. That cop couldn't have read my license plate. He never even got close to us. I just don't want to put the car back on the road while it's still dark."

"Come on," Sam said. "Tell me what's going on."

"It's all so rotten." Charlie took a deep breath. "You know Kate Bryant?"

"Yeah."

"We've been dating since before summer started."

"She's the girl you were talking about a year ago." Sam felt a twinge of jealousy similar to what he'd felt when Justin had told him about Tommy.

"She dumped me tonight."

"Really? Just like that?"

"Yep."

"Well, what did she say? She must have given you a reason."

Charlie dragged a hand through his hair. "Yeah, she gave me a reason."

Silence. Sam leaned his head forward. "It's a big secret?"

"It should be."

"Come on. Pretend we're the only two people on

the planet," he said. "Nobody but us."

"You'll freak out."

"No, I won't."

"All right, let me ask you something. Have you ever gotten high?"

The question caught Sam off guard. "You mean pot?"

"Such a model citizen," Charlie said. "Yes, I mean pot."

"No."

"Well, Kate's just as pure, if not more, as you are. And she doesn't want me doing it. But she found out that I do."

"You do? Since when?"

"Since about a year ago. Not a lot. Just sometimes. The point is, she doesn't want to go out with me anymore because of it."

"How'd she find out?"

"She just knew. I was dumb enough to call her when I was stoned, a couple of times. Plus, I kind of . . . stood her up. Like, a few days ago I was supposed to take her out for a nice dinner. She was all dressed up, waiting for me."

"Ouch."

"Yeah, that was a major screw-up."

"But you only do it sometimes?"

"I'm not keeping a written record, if that's what you're asking."

"Well, why don't you just stop doing it?"

"I could. I mean, I *can*. I'm going to. It's messed up my game, and I've been feeling like crap lately. But there's some serious stuff going on at home, and it helps sometimes, being able to . . . unwind."

"You know, I was really sorry about . . ." Sam didn't know how to finish the sentence in a way that would do any good; finally he just blurted it out. "Your mom. I heard she was sick, but I didn't know it was so serious. I was really sorry to hear what happened."

"Yeah." Charlie bent his head down. "It was pretty bad."

"I liked your mom."

"So did I." Charlie shook his head as if trying to dislodge a thought. "I haven't talked about it that much with anybody. No one really wants to hear about it, you know, when somebody dies who wasn't close to them. Unless they're a professional. Like that Ms. Rafferty, the guidance counselor? She called me in for an appointment, and we talked about it for twenty minutes. That was just . . . *weird*. She'd never even *met* my mom."

"What about your dad?"

"Forget it. He doesn't want to talk about it *at all*."

Sam nodded. "Maybe it's too upsetting."

"Of course it is. But I mean, we *never* talk about it. And he took down all my mom's pictures. It's almost like she never even existed. We haven't been out to the cemetery since, like, a month after she died."

"Well, what do you want him to say?"

"Anything! He could say that he misses her. He could say it totally sucks that she died. *Any*thing. But he just sits around, in a stupor. Plus he gets drunk almost every night."

"Really?"

"Yeah. I totally yelled at him tonight, and I shouldn't have because he was sober for once, but I'm tired of pulling all the weight around the house, you know? Why should he be drinking that much?"

"Maybe because he thinks *he* needs to unwind," Sam said.

The connection between his pot smoking and his dad's drinking had apparently never crossed Charlie's mind before. For a moment, his face leveled off to no expression whatsoever. Then Sam saw his jaw muscles tighten. "What's *he* got to unwind from?" Charlie asked sharply. "He isn't working. He never even leaves the house."

"I don't know. He still might feel like he needs to unwind."

"I didn't tell you about this so you could stick up for him."

"I'm not. I'm just saying maybe he has a reason. Like you do."

"He's got no reason to never talk about my mom—as if she didn't exist."

"Well . . . have *you* talked to *him* about her?"

"I can't! He'd get too upset. He'd start crying or something."

So, Sam thought, *maybe that's what needs to happen.* But he didn't say this because he didn't want to make Charlie more irritated than he already was. It was obviously a touchy subject.

"I'm just really sick of things the way they are,"

Charlie said, staring at his hands. "What a freakin' night."

"So are you going to tell me what happened to your car?" Sam asked, suddenly remembering the damage. "Nice car, by the way, except for how it's all banged up."

"Thanks. That was just . . . vandals."

"I thought you were going to say Kate did it, or your dad."

"No, no, no. It's totally unrelated to all that." Charlie got up and smacked his hands together. "Listen, it feels kind of strange, telling you all this. I mean, we're not exactly friends anymore, right?"

"I don't know," Sam said. "That was . . . a bad situation."

"Well, you did it, not me. So you ought to know. I'm still in the dark about that one."

"We could be friends again," Sam said cautiously. "Couldn't we?"

"Not unless you tell me what happened. I mean, how *can* we hang out together if I don't know what happened? Do you know how much time I spent wondering what the hell I did?"

"You didn't do anything," Sam said. "It was me, not you." He got up and started walking—but there was nowhere to walk but across the room, and then back again. He shoved his hands down into his pockets. "Could we maybe start over again? From this point? Start being friends again, and just forget about all that?"

Charlie shook his head no. An awful silence fell between them. But a few moments later, he exhaled and said, "Maybe. But you've got to admit, that's kind of weird."

"We'll just take a big eraser to it," Sam said. "We'll be like strangers. New planet, new friendship." He held out his hand. "Nice to meet you."

Charlie looked down at the hand, then back up at Sam's face. "So what were you so upset about, when you came running past the basketball court? You looked like you were out of your mind."

Sam lowered his hand.

"Remember? All that blabbering about leaving home and never coming back? What was that about?"

It was amazing that the events from earlier that evening had been able to recede to the back of Sam's mind. He'd barely given a thought to his mother, or Teddy, or Justin, from the moment he and Charlie had stepped into the Danforth house. He'd been completely absorbed by what Charlie had been telling him. But now his own predicament came flooding back. "We don't have to talk about that," he heard himself say in a weak voice.

"Man, where is your head? I just spilled my guts to you! And now you're not going to tell *me* what's going on?

How could he, knowing where the conversation would lead? "No."

"You're serious?"

"Yeah, I'm serious. I don't want to talk about it."

Charlie opened his mouth, but then just let it hang there without speaking, staring at Sam. "Get out of here," he said finally.

"What do you mean?" Sam asked, feeling his stomach tighten.

"I mean get out of here. I can't be your friend, Sam. I can't be friends with someone who's going to clam up about himself, who isn't going to *trust* me with what's going on in his life—especially not someone who already blew me off once."

"It's not about trust," Sam said.

"Whatever. That was a nice brand-new friendship. It was great for about two seconds. But it's over. Get out."

"You're kicking me out?" Sam asked. "After dragging me all the way out here?"

"I didn't drag you anywhere. You wouldn't have come if you didn't want to. Just get out. You can sleep on the porch, and I'll drive you back in the morning, but I don't want you in here."

"Charlie, that's not fair."

"*Fair?* I think it's *totally* fair. It doesn't feel too good, though, does it?"

"You don't understand."

"No, I don't. You know all about me, but I don't know a damn thing about you."

Sam looked around the empty room, as if it were filled with people and he were searching for someone who was on his side. "Come on. Don't do this."

"Out!" Charlie snapped. He pointed toward the glass door.

There was nothing to do but leave.

15.

(Would you shut up and tell me?)

Charlie paced the floor of the empty living room, furious.

What the hell was wrong with Sam? How hard could it be just to *talk* about what was going on? Granted, Charlie had clammed up around everybody in his life for the past year or so, but he would have been open with Sam, if they'd stayed friends. At least he thought so. He might not even be in the mess he was in with Derrick Harding if Sam hadn't trashed their friendship so abruptly. But then, he'd had that thought before, and he knew it led nowhere. He heard the echo of Kate's words: *You have to take some responsibility for your actions. You have to* own *some of this.*

What made him really mad, though, was that, out of the blue, he and Sam had had what felt like a solid chance of putting their friendship back together, and yet Sam couldn't even meet him halfway in their attempt to mend things. Charlie was angry at himself for opening up to someone who had turned into a sponge, soaking up other people's personal stuff and never giving anything back. That wasn't friendship. That was leeching. Maybe Sam, who was slated to be the new editor of the Cernak *Fountain* when school started up again, was turning into some kind of gonzo investigative reporter, collecting information. Charlie pictured an exposé about his life splashed across the front page of the first issue: BASKETBALL STAR TURNS POTHEAD, FIGHTS WITH DRUNKEN FATHER, LOSES GIRL.

He walked over to the sliding glass door at the back of the house and saw that Sam wasn't on the back porch. For a moment, Charlie wondered if he'd just left—if he'd hoofed it back through the palm scrub and was standing out on A1A now with his thumb raised, trying to hitch a ride . . . somewhere, since he didn't want to go back home.

Why didn't Sam want to go home? What had happened? It was eating at Charlie, and the very fact that he cared made him even angrier. Then he spotted a dark shape, far out on the beach: Sam, sitting cross-legged, facing the ocean. *To hell with him*, he thought. But that suddenly brought back to his mind the stupid game he'd come up with the night he was stoned on the basketball court. Smacking the ball against the wall, trying to hammer out every person in his life. The black eye he'd given himself. Maybe he wasn't quite the island he wanted to be.

After thinking about this for a few minutes, he grunted, grabbed the canvas tarp off the floor, and pulled open the glass door.

He felt the warm air move across the sweat that coated his arms and neck. The sand was an eerie shade of blue, almost neon, ribboned with wet streaks and stretching on for what seemed like miles. He followed the trail of Sam's footprints, and he cleared his throat to announce himself as he got closer, but Sam just kept facing the distant, rolling whisper of the surf. He'd taken off his running shoes and socks. They were sitting beside him.

Charlie kicked off his own shoes and unfolded the tarp. It was stiff with dried paint, but it would be better than sitting on damp sand. He sank down onto half of it and smacked the other side. "Sit on this before you soak your jeans."

"They're already soaked."

"Well, sit on it, anyway."

Sam didn't move.

"You know," Charlie said, "you're not going to be able to stay here."

"So you own the beach now?"

"No, I mean *here*." He pointed at the sand. "This spot will be about six feet under water when the tide comes in."

"Oh," Sam said. "Duh. I know that."

"Well, just sit on the damn tarp, would you? I know you're angry. I'm angry, too. Let's clear the air, and then we never have to talk again, *ever*. Okay?"

Sam looked over at the empty stretch of tarp. He looked up at Charlie. Then he lifted his body and scooted like a crab several feet to the left until he was sitting on the tarp. He dusted his hands together and refolded his arms over his knees, staring back out at the Atlantic. "So clear the air."

Charlie just breathed for several moments, trying to control his anger. "I really need you to tell me one thing. Just one thing."

"What," Sam said flatly.

"Why did you stop being my friend?"

"You really want to know?"

"I'm *telling* you I want to know."

"Because of Chris Kovan."

Charlie's mind drew a blank. "Who's Chris Kovan?"

"He used to go to Cernak," Sam said, still staring forward. "He moved to New Mexico last year."

Tall and loud, Charlie remembered. Used to work in the school store. "The gay guy?"

He heard the air rush out of Sam's mouth. "Yeah. The gay guy. Nicely put, only that wasn't what you called him when he was still living here."

"What did I call him?"

"A fag."

"Well, so what? Wait a minute . . . were you

friends with that guy, or something? I never saw you hang out together."

"We didn't. I hardly knew him. Neither did you. We just saw him sitting in the commons one day, and you said, 'That guy's such a fag.'"

"What's that got to do with us?"

Sam's bare feet were sticking out beyond the end of the tarp. He gouged his heels into the wet sand. "I didn't want to *hear* it, okay? It *offended* me."

"Well . . ." Charlie's mind jumped from thought to thought, wanting to say the right thing. "It's not like I'm a racist or anything."

"I'm gay," Sam said suddenly.

"No, you're not."

"What do you mean, no, I'm not?"

The response had just fallen out of Charlie's mouth. It seemed impossible that Sam was gay. He didn't talk gay. He didn't *act* gay.

"I know what I am. I know what I like. I could lie to you and say I'm confused, or bi, or whatever, but I'm not confused. I'm gay. I've never said that to another living person, but there it is. And it's the truth."

"Just slow down. I told you I've been smoking

pot, okay. But you don't have to try to one-up me with this gay thing."

"See how good I am at hiding it?" Sam said, turning to look at him. "You had no idea. The day you made that comment about Chris Kovan, I think I even made some comment back. Something like 'Yeah, he's a real homo.' I shouldn't have, but I did, because I didn't want you or anyone else to know what I was. But it told me how you feel about gay people."

"So you're mad at me for saying that?" Charlie said, digging his own feet into the sand. "You'd never said anything about it before, so how was I supposed to know? I made a crack, I said a dumb thing. Okay. But it's not like you were a black guy and I said something racist to your face."

"No, but what if I were a black guy who looked white? You could have easily said something. And that would have pissed me off, too."

"This is like science fiction," Charlie said. "I mean, what if I make a crack about alligators around some guy on the basketball team, and then he unzips his human suit and he's really an alligator? Is that my fault? I mean, how am I supposed to know something that's a total secret from the world?"

"I don't know," Sam said, looking down at his hands clasped together over his knees.

"So you ended our friendship over *that*? Without even telling me what I'd done wrong?"

"No, that was just part of it," Sam said. "There's more." He hesitated. He looked at Charlie, then looked away again. Instead of telling him what the 'more' was, he said, "I feel like a total freak around my family now. And something awful happened tonight. That's the only reason I stopped when I saw you. I was just really upset about something."

"You obviously want to tell me about it."

"You don't want to hear it."

"Don't tell me what I don't want to hear," Charlie snapped. "That's what you did the last time. Or you *assumed* it, without even giving me the chance to react. I want to hear!"

"My mom and dad are split up. Did you know that? My dad's living up in Ponte Vedra Beach with this guy, David. They're a couple. Like, a *couple*. And my mom isn't too happy about it, as you might imagine. She's got this awful boyfriend, Teddy, who's practically moved into our house, and he's always making these homophobic remarks, and the other day she asked me point-blank if I was gay, and I told her no. I lied to her face."

"Wait a minute," Charlie said, trying to keep up. "You're telling me your *dad's* gay?"

"Yeah. Isn't that a riot? Can't you just hear the talk? Sam Findley's dad's a homo, and he's turned Sam into one, too. There's all kinds of twisted stuff going on over at the Findley house."

"Whoa," Charlie said. "Why don't you stop putting words in everybody's mouth and just tell me what happened? I mean, tonight. What happened tonight that had you so freaked out?"

"I'm such a dumbass," Sam said, and rubbed a hand against his eyes.

"It's all right."

"It's not all right! I met this great guy a couple of weeks ago, and we went out on a date tonight. Can you imagine that? Me, on a date? I've never been on a date with anyone in my whole life. And Justin— this guy—he seemed to really like me. And so—this is going to totally gross you out . . ."

"Shut up," Charlie said. "Just tell me."

"We were kind of . . . making out in his car, in my driveway. And my mom saw us."

"Wow. She saw you? With this guy? Like that?" Charlie's own problems suddenly seemed a little less earth-shattering compared to all of this. But he made himself say, "It's not the end of the world, Sam."

"I flipped out!" Sam cried. "I didn't want her to see us, and I didn't even want to *look* at Justin, so I shoved him, and practically fell out of his car, trying to get away from them both. I just *ran*. How pathetic is that? Why would he ever want to talk to me again? He's got to think I'm the biggest freak in the universe. And my mom's probably thrown all my stuff out into the front yard by now."

"You know," Charlie said, "you've got a real bad habit of thinking you know everything that's in other people's heads. It's probably not as bad as you think."

"It's worse," Sam said. He sniffed and lifted his head. He stared out at the water. "Do you have any idea what it's like, screwing up so bad that your whole life just feels ruined?"

Charlie sat quietly for a moment. He pinched the front of his T-shirt and snapped it away from his chest, stirring the warm air. He said, "Let's walk."

They carried their shoes. Charlie carried the tarp, thrown over one shoulder. They walked out as far as they could, until the coastline was nothing but a string of tiny, scattered house lights and their feet were splashing through the water; then they followed the waterline.

He wanted to tell Sam everything now. He talked about his mom, her illness, how slowly she'd gotten sick, and how quickly she'd slid downhill. He didn't cry as he spoke, and he realized how good it felt just to be saying it out loud: His mom was gone, she was never coming back, and it made him sad every day of his life.

"You know," Sam said, "you should just be up front with your dad. Tell him you want to talk about her. Tell him you want to go out to the cemetery."

"I know I should. But he'll get so upset. And he'll probably start drinking even more."

"So he gets upset. As far as the drinking goes, that's

got to be dealt with anyway. He should get some help. But it's normal to be upset when someone dies, right?

"Yeah."

"So you have to talk to him. He can't read your mind."

"Thankfully."

"I can't read it either."

"Meaning what?"

"Meaning, you still haven't told me what really happened to your car."

"Well, that's a whole nother story. . . ."

Then he told Sam about Derrick Harding and the money he owed him. When he said the amount, Sam's jaw dropped.

"How do you smoke five hundred dollars' worth of pot?"

"Like this," Charlie said. He held two fingers up to his lips and sucked in air. "It wasn't that hard."

He told Sam why he was in the electronics store that afternoon trying to return his stereo. And about the envelope he'd stuffed under Derrick's door. Then he told him about Derrick and Wade coming over to the house and smashing up his car.

"They did that *tonight*?"

"Yeah. I tried to stop them, but they tore out of there before I could."

"Wait—what color car does Derrick drive?"

"Silver. An Eclipse. But I've already ruled out retaliation, if that's what you're thinking."

"We saw them! Justin and I saw them leaving the neighborhood. They must have been doing sixty."

"Sounds like them."

"You should call the police. I could be a witness to their getaway!"

"Hello? I don't *think* that cop got my license plate tonight, but what if he did? The police would be really interested in getting their hands on me and Derrick both. Plus, if they got hold of him and worked him over, he'd squeal about me being a regular customer. Speaking of which—" He stopped, dug the Baggie out of his pocket, and opened it. He turned it over, and the ocean breeze scattered it over the sand.

"That was pot?"

"That was pot."

"There are going to be some happy seagulls in the morning," Sam said. "You have this whole gangster life I didn't even know about."

"Well, what about you? You have this whole . . . gay life."

"In my mind, maybe."

"I had no idea," Charlie said.

"I think I'd rather have the gangster life."

"No, you wouldn't. Wait, I take that back. I don't want to tell you what you think. But believe me, it stinks. So what are you going to do about your mom?"

Sam kicked along the water for a few steps. He shrugged. "Nothing, because I'm never going home."

"Okay, and if we leave the Planet Sam for a moment and come back to Earth, what are you going to tell her?"

"What would *you* tell her?"

"That I was gay." It felt weird, saying the words, but it made him feel closer to Sam's predicament. "I'd just tell her I was gay, and that she was going have to get over it."

"I already lied to her."

"Well, there's nothing you can do about that now,

unless they have time machines on the Planet Sam. So you tell her you lied because you were worried she would flip out."

"She *is* going to flip out."

"I don't think it's really going to shock her, Sammy. Not after what she saw tonight. It could even work in your favor. It's like she saw the preview for the movie, so she sort of knows what to expect."

"You know one thing I want to do," Sam said. "I want to tell Teddy to shut his mouth."

"I would."

"He can *think* whatever he wants. But he doesn't have to say it around me. I mean, it's my house, right? I've got more claim to it than he has. And he's going to have to just . . . *behave* differently around me."

"If I was your mom," Charlie said, "I'd be proud of you for saying that."

"*Proud?* Are you crazy?"

"I'd be proud. I'd say, 'That's my gay son, Sam!'"

"Shut up!" Sam reached over and shoved Charlie sideways, splashing water over Charlie's ankles.

They were both laughing now. Charlie shoved him back, and Sam teetered as he tried to right himself, then fell over into the water.

"Oops," Charlie said.

"Oops, my ass," Sam said. He reached up and grabbed the tarp slung over Charlie's shoulder, as if using it to pull himself up. Then he yanked on it. Charlie went down.

They were sitting in the water, less than a foot apart. Sam dragged a hand over his face, pushing his wet hair out of his eyes. "Great," he said. "Really great. This is just what I needed."

"Actually, it feels kind of good," Charlie said, still laughing. He wiped at his eyes and spit off to the side. "Refreshing."

"You really are nuts, you know that? All that pot has made your head mushy."

"Maybe," Charlie said. "Let me ask you something, since we're clearing all this air. Have you told your dad you're gay?"

"No!" Sam wiped the salt water from his eyes. "How can I do that with so much else going on?"

"Well, think about it. How many gay guys have a gay dad they can talk to—you know, just to . . . sound things out? It's like finding out you're an alien, and then finding out your dad's an alien, too."

"Thanks."

"Sorry, that didn't come out right. All I'm saying is, it could be cool. He's certainly not going to throw your stuff on the lawn. Not that your mom is. I really think this could be okay, Sam. Weird for a little while, maybe. But people deal, you know?"

"Maybe." Sam looked down at his dripping hands. "Are we going to sit here in the water for the rest of the night, or can we go back to that house you kicked me out of?"

Charlie grinned. "Good idea."

Their wet clothes turned cool against their bodies during the walk back. When they got inside the house, Charlie turned on the gas heater and the thin bricks behind the wire mesh began to glow orange and warm the room. He took off his shirt and wrung it out in the kitchen sink, then draped it over a paint can in front of the heater. He told Sam to do the same.

"Think I'll keep mine on," Sam said.

"Well, come over here near the heat."

"It's ninety degrees outside."

"You still need to warm up. That water wasn't exactly boiling."

Charlie was already on his knees in front of the heater. Sam crossed the room and squatted down next to him.

They held their hands up, felt the warmth against their palms.

"You said there was something more," Charlie said after a while. He thought he was going to have to clarify this, but Sam seemed to know what he was talking about.

"Yeah."

"More than just that comment I made about Chris Kovan."

"There was."

"Well, here we are," Charlie said. "The air's getting pretty clear. You want to tell me now?"

"Not really."

Charlie shrugged. "Okay. Suit yourself."

"All right, I'll tell you," Sam said, "but if you freak out, don't blame me. I mean, I took care of it, it's not like I didn't do anything about it—"

"Would you shut up and tell me?"

"I think for a while, there, I . . . kind of had a crush on you."

Charlie had expected anything but this. He'd thought that whatever it was, it was about Sam and Sam's own stuff. He was surprised—and, in an odd way, glad—to find out he was a part of it. "On *me*?"

"Yeah. Go figure that one."

"What does that even mean? You know I'm straight, right?"

"Of course! That's what made it so difficult."

"Difficult like how? You never tried to do anything. Did you?"

"No!"

Slowly, carefully, Sam began to recount that night over a year ago when he'd gone to Charlie's tent in the backyard with the intention of running away, and how they'd talked and gone to sleep side by side. "Only I didn't sleep. I *couldn't* sleep. I almost kissed you."

"Shut up!" Charlie said. "Are you serious?"

"I *almost* did. I was about to do it, then I stopped myself, and you woke up. You remember that?"

"No. I remember you coming to the tent, that's all."

"It scared the hell out of me. I didn't want it to happen again and didn't know what else to do. It just would have been weird and . . . difficult . . . being around you and thinking about you that way. And if you'd found out, you would have freaked."

Charlie was silent, staring into the heater.

"I'm right, aren't I?" Sam asked. "It would have totally weirded you out."

"Sure. Totally," Charlie said. And Sam was right: He would have freaked if something like that had happened. "But only for a while. I don't think I would have ended our friendship over it. It's kind of flattering, in a way." He blinked and looked at Sam.

"You would have punched my lights out."

"Shut up! I would not. . . . Okay, maybe I would have popped you one. But you would have had it coming to you, taking advantage of a guy in his sleep. So what about now? Are you still worried about it?"

"Oh, I'm over you."

"Thanks a lot!"

Sam laughed. "Well, it's not like you're some kind of love god. I just got past it, that's all."

"You and Kate both, apparently."

"I'd hardly compare those two situations."

"Wait, there's still something I don't get. If you knew I was straight, why'd you want to kiss me? I mean, you knew it wasn't going to go anywhere."

"Of course I knew that. It doesn't mean I didn't want to do it. You'd just been telling me all that stuff about how, if you really like someone, you owe it to yourself to at least try. 'Sometimes you've just got to lean over and plant one on their lips,' you said. 'If you're not bold, you'll never know.'"

"I said all that?"

"*Yes*. You practically pushed me to it without even realizing it. I knew it wasn't going to lead any-where. I'm not stupid. I just wanted to do it once, and the idea made me a little crazy, all right?"

Charlie was nodding his head. He was thinking—not about that night in the tent, but about how awful it had been not having Sam for a friend over the past year. "So you ended our friendship because you wanted to kiss me? Knowing there was no chance—"

"Well, yeah. I guess it sounds kind of stupid, but yeah. It was all I could think to do."

Charlie stopped nodding. Another thought came into his head. Funny, weird, impulsive. It had already been such a crazy night so . . . what the hell? He leaned over and kissed Sam square on the mouth—not a make-out kiss, but not a peck, either. Something in between.

When he pulled his head back, he could feel himself starting to grin. "There," he said. "Now you know."

Sam looked astounded. After a moment, he said, "Why did you do that?"

"Because you wanted to find out what it was like. Don't go über-gay on me, or anything. We're not going to get hot and heavy; that was a one-shot deal. But why not? You were my best friend, Sam. I've really missed you."

Sam seemed to be staring right through him. He still looked shocked. Then he said, "That was really cool."

"You're not going to faint or anything, are you?"

"No, I mean it's really cool that you just did that."

"And I'm still alive to talk about it. So . . . what did you think?"

"Of the kiss?"

Charlie shrugged. "Yeah."

Sam looked at the heater for a moment, then said, "Sorry. Justin McConnell's a better kisser."

Charlie shoved him sideways, and Sam rolled onto the floor, laughing. He came to rest on his back, and his laughter slowly died out. In a heavier voice, he said, "This is probably the best and the worst day I've ever had."

"It's up there," Charlie said. "And down there. I wouldn't say it's the worst, but I sure didn't see my summer ending up this way."

"Me either. When did we turn into such screwups?"

"We're not screwups," Charlie said, really wanting to believe it about himself. "We're not saints, and we're not screwups. We're just . . . people."

"So what do we do now?"

His mind moved in several different directions at once. There was just too much to think about. Charlie yawned, dragged a hand through his hair, and said, "Damage control."

16.

Early the next morning, the banged-up Volkswagen rolled to a stop in front of the Findley residence. Sam got out of the car, crossed his fingers in a good-luck gesture to Charlie, and walked reluctantly toward the house. It was Sunday. His mom's car was in the driveway. Teddy's wasn't. Sam unlocked the front door as quietly as possible and stepped inside.

She was sitting at the dining-room table. She wasn't reading the newspaper. She wasn't even drinking a cup of coffee. She was in her robe with her arms folded, waiting for him.

"I know you want to kill me," Sam said, "but can you kill me later? I really need to get some sleep."

"No," his mom said. "Sit down."

He and Charlie had stayed up all night talking. He felt exhausted and grimy, and sitting down at the table with his mom was about the last thing in the world he wanted to do. But there was no use arguing. He took the chair across from her. "Where's Hannah?"

"She's still in bed."

His mom looked angry. She looked exhausted, too. She probably hadn't slept, probably had sat up all night thinking about her gay ex-husband and her gay son, wondering if she'd done anything to cause it all. She was about to blow her top, he thought.

But when she spoke, her voice was oddly calm. "The first thing I want to know is if you're all right."

"I'm fine."

"Where have you been?"

"With Charlie."

"Charlie Perrin?"

"Yeah. I sort of . . . ran into him after I left here. We hung out and talked for a while. I think we patched up our friendship."

"You know it's not okay to spend the entire night away from the house like that, without telling anyone where you are."

"I know."

"I was half out of my mind, worried that you'd gone off the deep end and were going to try to hurt yourself—"

"I'd never do that," Sam said.

"Well, how would I know, when you just disappeared?" she shot back. She took a deep breath, exhaled, and leveled her voice again. "The second thing I want to know is whose car that was I saw you in. Who was that person you were with?"

"Can I please just go to bed?"

"*No.*"

Sam's hands started to fidget. He put them under the table. "His name is Justin."

"Justin who?"

As if it mattered now. "Justin McConnell."

"He lives around here?"

Sam nodded. "He just transferred to Cernak."

With her initial round of questions out of the way, his mother seemed more tired now than angry.

She ran her eyes over the bare table. After what felt like an eternity, she looked up and asked, "Why did you lie to me?"

"About what?" Sam knew about what, but he didn't want to answer. Her gaze was fixed on him now, piercing him like a pin through an insect.

"You know about what."

"Because I didn't want to tell you," he said.

"Why?"

"*Because.* You *know* why. I was worried about how you'd react. I was scared."

"I want you to tell me honestly—is this something you're testing out? You know, experimenting with? Or is it something you think is . . . set in stone?"

"Mom, I don't know." If there was ever a time to be truthful and just pour it out on the table, it was now. "It wasn't a *whim*, if that's what you mean. It's something I've always felt, or felt for a long time, anyway." He looked up at her. "Dad has nothing to do with this."

"I wonder."

"What's that supposed to mean?"

"It means, I wonder if it was an idea that wasn't in your head at all, before your father moved out. Maybe that's what put it there."

"*No.* That's what I'm saying. It didn't just . . . pop into my head. It was always there."

"And you're sure of that?"

How long could they talk around the word without using it? "Yes. I'm gay, Mom. I could lie to you again, or tell you I think I might be, but I *am*."

"So you jumped out of that car and ran away because of how you thought I'd react?"

"Yes."

"You know, that boy sat in our driveway for a long time."

Sam felt his heart jump. An awful image suddenly flashed in his mind: his mom and Justin sitting down together to hash this thing out. "Did you talk to him?"

"No. He sat out there in his car for about fifteen minutes, though. Then he left."

Sam breathed a sigh of relief.

"You said his name is Justin?"

"Uh-huh."

"Do his parents know about him?"

"I don't know. Can we not talk about him right now? I'm embarrassed enough to drop dead as it is."

"Well, I wish you hadn't run off like that, Sam. And frankly, I'm very mad at you for lying to me. We wouldn't have had all this drama if you'd told me the truth the other day."

"How could I do that? Teddy walks around here making cracks about gays and you don't seem to care at all. Why should that make me feel like I can tell you the truth?" Sam glanced into the adjoining living room. "He's not here now, is he?"

His mom folded her arms over her stomach. "No." She took several deep breaths, then said, "He won't be for a while."

"Why?"

"We had a . . . conversation last night that bothered me."

"A fight?" Sam asked.

"You could call it that. After you ran off, and after that boy drove away, I went in and told Teddy what had happened."

"You *told* him? Why'd you do that?"

"Because I'm tired of *secrets*. Your father and I did nothing but keep secrets from each other for the last two years of our marriage, and look where it got us. We would have separated anyway, but if we'd been up front with each other about things, maybe there would have been a lot less fighting."

"What secrets did *you* have?" Sam asked hesitantly.

"Just about the way I was feeling. Things weren't that great between us anymore, and I was pretending like they were and hiding from him the way I really felt. It wasn't good. And then last night it was clear that you had this big secret you were keeping from me, so big that I had to find out by spying through the front window and you had to go running off into the night. I just didn't like the idea of getting back into bed, in my own house, with one more secret nobody was supposed to talk about."

"So you told *Teddy*? You know how he feels about stuff like that. He makes it really obvious."

"Well, that's his mistake, shooting his mouth off like that. And it was my mistake to let him do it. If I'd known—about you, I mean—I would have made him stop a long time ago. I owe you an apology for that."

Sam was caught off guard. He certainly didn't expect his mother to be apologizing to *him* for anything. "O-okay."

"So there's Teddy's mistake, my mistake, and yours. But we all make mistakes, and I know that. What matters is what you do when you *find out* you've made a mistake. Teddy should have found out quick, when I told him. It's called rising to the occasion. But, well, Teddy didn't do that."

"What did he say?"

"I'm not going to tell you. He said some stupid things and he wouldn't take them back. So he left pretty early this morning."

"You kicked him out?" Sam asked, trying to suppress the hint of happiness in his voice.

"I asked him to leave. He'll probably call here in a few days, and if he does and you pick up, don't get into anything with him. And don't *start* anything, either. Just call me to the phone, all right?"

"All right. Are you still going to see him?"

"I don't think so. But that's not your fault. Listen, you're sure about this thing? Being gay, I mean.

Because life is hard enough without choosing to make it harder, Sam. There are things you're going to have to be ready for if—"

"I know what you're talking about."

"Maybe you don't. You're barely seventeen years old; you don't know everything yet. But what I'm trying to say is, you don't have to decide . . . what you are . . . right now."

"I didn't decide it, Mom. I didn't choose it. I think it's just who I am."

"All right, then." She brought the heels of both hands up and rubbed them into her eyes. "If I don't get some sleep soon, I'm going to snap," she said. When she brought her hands down, Sam saw that she was crying.

He was scared. He felt like he'd caused all of this, like he was doing nothing but more harm just by sitting here at the table. "Don't cry, Mom. It's okay."

"I know that. This is just going to take some getting used to. There's nothing I can do about it. I can't speed things up, so you're going to have to be patient with me. In fact, you're going to have to *work* with me on this."

"I will," Sam said.

"I don't want you hiding some huge part of yourself from me. If you start doing it now, it'll just get easier and you'll never stop. We'll be strangers by the time you're twenty. I don't want that to happen. Understand?"

"Yeah," Sam said.

"Good. Now go get some sleep."

"I'm sorry I worried you." He started to get up from the table. Then he hesitated. "I love you, Mom."

"I love you, too." She wiped her eyes with the sleeve of her robe.

"I might be going over to Charlie's later this afternoon."

"No, you won't."

Sam stopped in the doorway. "Why not? I told you, he and I have kind of patched things up."

"And I'm glad. But you're grounded," she said. "For staying out all night. Did you think that was a freebie?"

"No, but—grounded for how long?"

She shrugged. "A week."

"Come on, Mom, I said I was sorry."

"You're sorry and I'm sorry. I'm still the parent

here. A week. I'll grant you phone privileges, how's that? You can call Charlie, and Melissa—and whoever else you might want to call."

Did she mean Justin?

"All right." Sam groaned. But he didn't feel so bad. A little bewildered, maybe. Exhausted, definitely. But not so bad. He turned and walked back to his room.

He slept until after four in the afternoon. Not long after he got up, he heard a low thumping on his bedroom door, as if someone were gently kicking it from the other side.

"Come in."

"I don't have any hands."

He got up and opened the door, and Hannah stepped into the room carrying a tray with a sandwich and a glass of milk. "I made you this. You have to eat lunch before it's dinnertime," she said.

"Hey, thanks."

She set the plate and the glass down on his nightstand. "Did you notice I knocked?"

"You kicked."

"Better than just opening the door."

"You're right. Thanks for that, too." He took a bite from the sandwich.

"Mom says you're grounded."

"Good news travels fast. Why'd she tell you that?"

"Because I asked her if she'd take us to the movies, and she said you couldn't go. What are you grounded for?"

"I stayed out too late last night. Really late. And Mom stayed up wondering where I was. So she's awake now?"

"Yeah, but she took a humongous nap this afternoon. How's the sandwich?"

"Great," he said around a mouthful of bologna.

"I didn't want you to starve in here."

"I'm not grounded to my *room*. I can walk around the house if I want to."

"Oh. Can I wear your jean jacket?" She was staring into the open mess of his closet.

"Sure," he said.

It was like he'd given her a ten-dollar bill in a candy shop. "Thanks!" She yanked the jacket off its hook and darted out of the room.

Sam finished eating, then carried the dishes into the kitchen.

His mom was in the living room on the sofa, reading. He picked up the cordless phone from the coffee table. "Do you need this?" he asked.

"No. Go ahead." She still looked sleepy, but she didn't look angry anymore. "Melissa called while you were asleep."

"Thanks. That's who I was going to call."

Back in his room, he dialed Melissa's number. As he did, he thought about how tempting it was just to be honest with her, come clean. *I'm not ready to do it,* he thought. He heard the phone ringing at the other end of the line.

Why am I not ready?

It rang again.

Because I'm not. That's all there is to it. Maybe next summer, when school is over and done with.

Another ring.

Is that the best excuse you can come up with?

Melissa picked up the phone, obviously having looked at the caller ID. "Hi! So tell me how it went! I've been totally distracted today, wondering. I thought you were going to call last night, but no. You left me, your good friend, completely in the dark about this grand tourist adventure with—"

"I'm gay," Sam said. It was like a pressure valve suddenly blew somewhere inside his head.

There was a brief pause. *"What?"*

"I was lying the other day. I knew you wouldn't care, one way or another, but I lied. And I apologize. I'm gay."

"Wow," Melissa said. A few moments later, she said, "Wow" again.

"Yeah," he said. "Wow."

"I feel like I'm getting a major exclusive here."

"Not so exclusive, as it turns out," Sam said. By his count, Melissa was the fifth person to find out his big secret in the past twenty-four hours.

He told her everything. Well, *almost* everything. The only detail he left out was the kiss Charlie had given him. Not all secrets were bad, and he knew Charlie would want that one to stay between the two of them. As for the rest, he spelled it out step-by-step, right through the conversation he'd had with his mom early that morning.

When he was finished, Melissa said, "Thank you."

Sam almost laughed. "For what? Dumping all my problems in your lap?"

"For telling me. I feel really honored that you trust me."

"I've always trusted you, Melissa. I was just, I don't know, uncomfortable."

"No reason to be," she said. "Please, someday I'll tell you what's *really* going on in my head, and you'll find out what a major weirdo I am."

"Like I don't already know that."

"It's why we get along so well, I guess. So what are you going to do about Justin?"

"Crawl under a rock and die," Sam said.

"That won't exactly fix the situation."

"There's nothing to fix. Besides, I can't even think about it right now. I just wanted to catch you up on things."

"I'm glad you did. Hey, does this mean I've been demoted? Has Charlie moved back up to your best-friend slot?"

"I think I can have more than one of those," he said, suddenly feeling very lucky.

After they had said good-bye, Sam sat, thinking. He suddenly smelled the ocean in his room. It took him a minute to realize it was coming from *him*, from having rolled around in the salt water with Charlie. His hair, when he reached up and touched it, felt stiff and dry.

He took a long, hot shower. He thought about everything that had happened and everything that Charlie had told him. So much of what they had confided in each other still seemed up in the air, unresolved.

Back in his room, he got dressed and dialed Charlie's number, surprised that he still had it memorized.

Mr. Perrin answered.

"Hi, Mr. Perrin. It's Sam. Findley."

"Sam Findley," Mr. Perrin said, as if he'd never heard the name before. And then, "Sam! How are you, Sam? I can't remember the last time I laid eyes on you. It must be, what, at least a year."

"Not since—" Sam stopped himself. Then, remembering what he'd talked about with Charlie, he said gently but deliberately, "Not since before

Mrs. Perrin passed away. I was really sorry to hear about that. I always liked her."

"Well." Mr. Perrin cleared his throat. "Well," he said again. "Mrs. Perrin always liked you, too, Sam."

"I'm sorry for your loss." Sam had no idea what was the *right* way to talk about someone who had died. But he thought he shouldn't shy away from it with Mr. Perrin. "She always seemed so happy with you and Charlie. She was a happy person, I mean. Anybody would be lucky to have such a good family." *Okay*, he told himself, *shut up now.*

But Mr. Perrin said, "You know what, Sam? I think you're right. She *was* happy. Sometimes I forget to be glad about that." There was a heavy sadness in his voice. But he sounded almost glad to be talking about his wife. "I wish she were here now, she'd love to hear your voice. She always said you and Charlie were the kind of friends who would know each other for a lifetime."

"Well, we're working on that. Is Charlie there?"

"Oh, of course, hold on a second." Mr. Perrin's voice moved away from the phone. "Charlie! It's Sam!"

A few moments later, Charlie came onto the line. Sam heard the click of Mr. Perrin hanging up his extension. "What's up?" Charlie asked. "Did you survive your mom's wrath?"

"Yeah. It wasn't that bad, actually."

Charlie said, "Right."

"Okay, it was horrible. But I'm not dead, so that's a good sign, right?"

"I guess so. You told her?"

"Well, I didn't exactly have to, did I?" He gave Charlie some of the highlights of the conversation with his mom, then told him about how Teddy was, at least for the moment, out of the picture.

"That's a saving grace," Charlie said.

"I'm just glad he wasn't here when I got back this morning. Did you tell your dad about what happened to the car?"

"*No.* He hasn't been outside or even looked out the front window, though, so it hasn't come up."

"Good."

"He'll notice it tomorrow for sure, because I'll have to move the VW so we can get the Buick out. We're going to the cemetery to visit my mom's grave."

"Really? How did you manage that?"

"I basically just told him we were going to do it. Isn't that weird? I said, 'Let's drive out to the cemetery tomorrow,' and he said, 'I don't think so, Charlie.' So I said, '*I* think so. I want to. I want to put some flowers on Mom's grave.' Then I said I'd go by myself if he didn't want to go with me. He got really quiet for a while. Then he said, 'All right, let's go.' It was that easy. I felt like I was putting my foot down, but I'd never just *asked* him before. I kept waiting for him to ask me."

"What are you going to tell him about your car?"

"That one I haven't figured out yet."

"Well, if you want, we can ride out to the junkyard together and try to dig up some taillights. Only I can't do it till Saturday, because I'm grounded."

"You got grounded? For making out with what's his name—Justin?"

"No! Strangely enough, it wasn't for that. It was for staying out all night."

"Lucky you, I guess. My dad didn't even notice I wasn't here. He slept the whole night through."

"Lucky *me*? I'd rather be in your shoes." Sam

remembered, then, why he'd called. "Listen, remember that money you owe Derrick Harding?"

Charlie grunted into the phone. "Like I could forget it."

"You're going to fight me on this, but I'm not going to take no for an answer. I have at least that much sitting in the bank."

"So?"

"So take it! Get this creep off your back."

"No," Charlie said firmly. "I'll work this out on my own."

"Save the macho act. It's me you're talking to. I've been working all summer, basically getting paid to be out of the house and away from Teddy—who isn't even around now. Seriously, I have more than enough socked away. What am I going to do with it? Buy three iPods? I don't need it right now, so you should take it."

"No way. *Thanks*, but no way. I need to be responsible for my own actions."

"Charlie, this makes complete sense. Who knows what this guy's going to do the next time he comes around for a payment? For all you know, he could come back this afternoon. If you want, you can consider it a loan and pay me back over the next year. But really, if you do this, you'll erase Derrick Harding from your life in a heartbeat."

"Sam, this isn't your problem."

"I know that. And it won't be a problem for me to lend you the money, either."

There was a long pause. Sam heard Charlie breathing through the phone line. Finally, Charlie said, "I'd want to pay you interest."

"You're so macho. Fine. Pay me interest. Pay me whatever interest the bank would pay me, if I left it sitting there. How's that?"

"Well . . . thanks."

"Don't thank me. Or if you *have* to thank me somehow, just so you can sleep at night, you can come over and clean my room once a week."

"I'm not touching *that* pigsty."

"How soon they lose their gratitude," Sam said with an affected air. "Have you talked to Kate?"

"About what? She dumped me. I told you that."

"I know. I was just wondering if you'd tried to do a little—"

"Damage control? I don't know if there's any hope of that at this point. She thinks I'm a total drug addict."

"Well, you're not. And she's a smart person, right? Isn't she in, like, every brainiac club in the school?"

"Practically."

"So she's smart enough to know you screwed up. Everybody screws up now and then. Tell her you've gotten your act together."

"It would take more than that. I'd have to prove it to her. She's a mondorealist, and she'd want hard evidence."

"So prove it. You can't do that?"

"Of course I can do that. The questions is, is she still even interested?"

"You won't know until you try."

"You're a little bossy, you know that? I think this was easier when you were all insecure and crushin' on me and I was oblivious."

"Those days are long gone, my friend." Sam was on a roll. It was fun talking to Charlie like this. He felt like *he* was teaching him how to make a particular shot on the basketball court. "It's all about the now. You line up for your best shot, and you take it. Nothing but net. Woosh."

"Or swish, in your case."

"The interest on your loan just went up."

"Hey! I was kidding! Can't I kid you about this, or is it off limits?"

"You can kid me," Sam said. "I may have to kick your ass at some point, but you can kid me."

"Good luck with that one, Findley. So are you going to call this guy again, or what?"

"Who? Justin? I'm too mortified to even think about that."

"You ought to call him. You're going to be seeing him in school in a couple of weeks, and think how weird *that's* going to be if you haven't talked since last night."

"You and I managed not to say a word to each other at school for a whole year."

"Yeah, and it wasn't exactly a joyride, was it? Not for me, anyway. Call him. I know you like this guy a lot."

"Yeah. He's great. But I can't call him, Charlie. It's just too embarrassing."

"So e-mail him. It's perfect: If he wants to respond, he'll respond. If he doesn't, then at least you'll know it's because he didn't want to."

"Maybe." Sam wanted to change the subject. "So—the junkyard on Saturday?"

"Sounds good."

"It's great, you know, just talking to you. I'm actually glad all this crap happened, if it means we're friends again."

"Same here," Charlie said. "You make a rotten ex-friend."

"Thanks. I'll take that as a compliment."

After they hung up, Sam got dressed. He still felt tired from having been up all night, so he lay down on his bed to take a nap. But he couldn't fall asleep. His mind leapfrogged from Justin to Teddy, from Teddy to his mom, from his mom to Charlie, to his dad, to Melissa . . . to Justin. There was no harm in just sitting down at the computer, right? Click around on the keyboard, see what happened. Whatever he typed never had to leave the room.

He opened Justin's last e-mail and clicked reply.

So, he typed, *I'm the biggest jerk on the planet.*

He deleted this. He stared at the screen for a moment, then typed, *I know you probably think I'm the biggest jerk on the planet. If you'll do me the favor of just reading to the end of this e-mail, I'll be grateful no matter what you decide I am.*

Better, he thought. Less pathetic, anyway. More direct. He rested his fingers on the keyboard and tried to relax his mind and focus on what he really wanted to say.

> You might already know this, Justin, but going out with you yesterday was a huge step for me. You told me, when we were sitting in my driveway at the end of the night (right before I went psycho) that the whole day had kind of felt like a date to you. Well, it did to me, too. From the moment we first talked about getting together and doing something, I thought of it as a date, even though I told myself I didn't. The truth is, I *wanted* it to be a date, and it scared the hell out of me.
>
> I guess I've gotten used to hiding who I

am—sometimes even from myself. And I almost lost my best friend forever because of it (I'll tell you that story sometime, if we're even speaking to each other). The point is, I made up my mind that I wasn't going to do anything about it, ever.

He deleted the word *it* and typed *being gay*.

Then I met you. That sounds corny, but it's true. I met you and I thought, Wow, look at that guy. He's so together. He's so comfortable with who he is. Why can't I be like that? Never in a million years would I have thought that someone like you would want to hang out with someone like me, so when you asked me to, I about croaked on the spot. You have no idea how nervous I was.

But you know what? From the first minute, yesterday, I was comfortable around you. And more than that—I like you, Justin. In a way I never would have admitted to liking anyone before.

So why did I freak out?

I should treat this like a news story and just stick to the facts:

While we were kissing (which was incredible, by the way), I looked up at the house and saw my mom staring at us. I'm not out to her. Or I wasn't. I am now. I'm also out, as of this afternoon, to my best friend, my other best friend, and my mom's ex-boyfriend, if you can follow all that. But last night I wasn't out to anyone but you—and I hadn't even officially admitted that much. So I panicked. I'd do just about anything now to change what happened so that you didn't see me react like that, but I can't.

I'm sorry, Justin. I wish I hadn't run away. The fact that I even got into the situation to begin with tells me a lot about myself, and about you.

So where do we go from here? I guess that's up to you. I wouldn't blame you for never wanting to talk to me again. You seem like

the most confident guy in the world, but
maybe you weren't, always. Maybe you've
been where I am right now.
Respond if you want to. I hope you do.
Sam.

He read it over three times. He changed a few
words, but the message stayed the same. He might
run it by Melissa, see what she thought. He could
even run it by Charlie, if he felt like it, and the fact
that both of these things were options made it seem
as if the windows and the door to his room had all
been thrown wide open—in a good way. It was a
strange feeling. But what if Justin deleted it without
even reading it? Wouldn't that just add more embarrassment to the situation? Wouldn't it be better just
to cut his losses on this one, and move on?

The sun was intensely bright outside his window.
There really was nothing to lose at this point, and
there might be a whole lot to gain, if he was willing
to stick his neck out.

Sam moved the cursor across the screen, took a
deep breath, and clicked Send.